RINGS

Benjamin K Hewett

RINGS

ISBN-13: 978-1511985758

To Edward and Carlito, who told me to stop fooling around and get my stories out there.

When Magnus and I walked away from the Black Cat and a bad game of darts, I was already neck-deep in trouble.

You think sticking your knife in some fully-oathed assassin calls down bad Karma? Try declaring war on the whole bloody guild. . . . They might forgive a first offense—if you look promising—but there is no place safe in Teuron for a guy who's said he's going to hunt them all down one by one.

For the record, I never actually said that, and what I did say was taken grossly out of context.

But context won't buy you coffins, or keep you out of them. Even if I toss the truth out there, I'm still dead. It just hasn't happened yet.

Still, truth is sacred. Tonight, for instance. I bet a penny on a game of darts when I shoulda been buying a loaf for my kids. Betting a penny won't ruin your life, even if it is your last.

If it'd just been the penny—a queenpence to be precise—then I would have simply walked away and ditched this mess like a bad dream. I've had worse days, and it wouldn't have hurt my kids to miss a meal. Besides, I find pennies in all sorts of interesting places.

But it wasn't just the queenpence. Barkus called in my debt. As the proprietor of the Black Cat Tavern and Inn—home to the best game of darts (and least reputable clientele) in Ector—he's got more than enough ways to make things uncomfortable for a welcher.

So I slipped Magnus some black pomegranate and watched the chaos unfold. Chaos, because Lucinda and the town drunk tipped off a brawl when they figured out that Magnus suddenly couldn't see anymore. I'm not proud of it, but it isn't the worst thing that's happened in the Black Cat, even though things did get worse when the Northern Nightshade Convention rode into town, and not just the peons, but the top brass, too. And they didn't come to lower Ector to piddle about whose dagger was bigger than whose. They came for Magnus, whom I'd just intentionally blinded.

Sigh.

That's the problem with having a conscience: It keeps

a man poor and it puts him in the middle of messes better left untouched.

You've probably heard about how it turned out, too, with dead Nightshades lying all over the place, and Pale Tom setting the neighborhood ablaze in one angry burst of death-flame?

No?

Well that's not the worst of it, anyways. The worst of it began with guilt and the decision to put Magnus up for the night. Housing a half-blind paladin is all kinds of stupid, especially if said paladin has had a hand in "laying to rest" a few top Nightshades. Evenings like that don't stay nicely in the past.

I'm not saying I'd change anything: I'm just saying it wasn't very smart. But I'm getting ahead of myself.

When the fires are out—besides Lucinda's—I take Magnus back to my place. He can barely stand by the time we get home, and he's just happy to have a place away from the noise.

I pick the back lock—we lost the keys ages ago—and lead the way up the creaky wooden risers in the pitch-black and into the dark kitchen where I strike up a tallow candle.

I help Magnus settle into the most comfortable chair, a rocker. It's perfectly suited for this. Though the cobbler is gone, and the shop below has been shuttered since her passing, the rocker clicks on. With its gently oiled ash woodwork and sturdy runners, it has known its share of troubles. But nothing like this.

We get his boots off, tunic, trousers, everything, and man, he's a mess. Puncture wounds. Lacerations from Pale Tom's twin swords. Splinters. A rope burn. I have to trim and restack the last candle several times just to have enough light to get him cleaned up. Water. Alcohol. Clean rags.

The stitches I make aren't pretty, but they are functional, and my fingers ache when I'm done.

"Teacup," he says, "you're a champ. I didn't realize how bad things were."

I grit my teeth. Just one of these slices would've been

the end of me, going clean through the other side of my skinny ribs. *Pan's beard!*

"You need to be in bed." I help him up.

"Or in a grave," he mutters.

"You die now, you'd better replace the candle we just wasted, first."

Magnus chuckles. "I'll buy you more than that. We'll go shopping first thing in the morning."

I don't argue. It's not for pride's sake; it's 'cause he's standing on my toes. I try not to gasp. "Magnus, how much does a blind paladin weigh?" I'm well-constructed—as they say—but large is the enemy of small no matter how "well-constructed" one might be. And Magnus is definitely not small.

"Oops. Sorry."

"S'okay," I lie, feeling hot blood rush back into place. Running my hand through thick brown shocks of hair to distract myself from the pain, I watch as a strand of gray shakes loose and drifts to the floor. I'm too young for gray, but it's there anyways.

I also don't mention to Magnus that he's counting on Lucinda—a sworn pickpocket—to ferry his chubby purse of golden kings back from the Black Cat all by herself..

I pull the blanket up to his chin. It's been cooling

down more at night lately, and I don't want him catching cold on top of all his battle wounds.

He's sleeping like a baby long before my toes stop hurting. At least one of us is sleeping. And he deserves it.

I deserve it too, I decide, but someone has to wipe up the spilt blood pooling on the rough, plank floor near the long square rug that's soft on bare feet. Someone has to throw away used bandages, fetch new water for the morning, and wait up for foraging adolescents.

I pad down the stairs and out the back door, carrying the water bags to the nearest well, enjoying the stillness. My ears—sharp—have fun picking up the faint sounds of celebration still going on in the distance, echoing lightly between the wood-shingled, timber-framed, and white plaster houses. And something else. Halting footsteps, whispers on the midnight cobblestones.

Barking dogs.

The splashing of water being emptied to the street from upper windows.

The neighbor's mangy cat. *Rrrrrooooowwwwwllllll!*

The hair on my neck and arms stands up stiff just as a cold wind blows across my face. I get goose-flesh and I don't know why. It's the feeling I get when Pale Tom's prowling about. It's the crackle of a lightning storm on the green farming hills to the north of Ector, when your horse is lame and the assassins' guild is hot on your trail. It's the false friend of an autumn storm, when the air is wet and warm, but you know it for an illusion before the real storm: a cold—bitter cold—winter.

It's the feeling of danger.

I shiver to shake it off. I hate that feeling.

When I get back with the water, Magnus is snoring like a log and Timnus and Valery have joined him, crowding into the master bed and snuggling down. The bed is theirs by default—since I never use it—but they aren't picky. They know there's something special about Magnus, something safe and steady that can be felt in the rising and falling of his bellows-like chest.

At thirteen-years-old they barely fit: Valery, all legs, and Timnus with melon-sized elbows. Some nights they bicker over who is stealing all the covers and who is elbowing who in the ribs, but tonight they're as dead asleep as Magnus, smashed up tight against him, leaching his heat in the cool autumn night. Somehow they're all crowded in, and the blanket's covering everyone.

I'm not sure how they got in tonight. I would have seen them from the well if they'd come up the back stairs like Magnus and me. This isn't the first time, either. One

11

minute it's just me washing up, and the next minute they're there, staring at me with those luminous, not-so-innocent eyes. They always get in, even when I lock the door. I guess they're learning a useful trade. . . . Locksmithing, hopefully.

I'm just glad they're sleeping soundly on full tummies. The town's been celebrating ever since the fire went out and Pale Tom disappeared in flames and smoke. He's dead. That's for sure. I saw Magnus's shining sword pierce his cold heart before he exploded into stars and light. I miss him, even though I know he was as evil as they come. I can't help it. Of all the people in Ector, Pale Tom understood me from left earlobe down to right kidney, all from a single creepy glance and the rasp of his bone-saw breath.

But he's gone now, thanks to Magnus, and he's taken a clawful of Nightshades with him to boot, so he can't be all that bad.

Quiet.

Ah-hh.

The solitude is nice after a busy evening. I lather off the blood, soot, poison, and excess antidote from my nimble fingers and sun-browned forearms, cheap suds sliding into the cloudy water. . . . I'm practically asleep at

12

the water basin, dreaming of my soft straw pallet in the attic.

Knock. Knock.

Who, in Pan's name, is prowling about at this ungodly hour?

Knock. Knock.

I ghost down the stairs, hoping to keep the knocking from waking the neighbors, the kids, and Magnus.

It's Petri, Lower Ector's best bookie and fence. It's unusual to see him without his crutch or his bet-book. He smells like waste water and looks a bit worse for the wear, as if he'd been razzled by some toughs down 'round dockside. There's a splotch of blood on his lip and a dark bruise on his left cheek, one that's obvious in the cloudy moonlight.

He pokes his tongue through the gap in his teeth and bobs his head like a magpie trying to impress someone. I can tell he's trying to see up my stairs. I close the door a little more, making it seem like I'm just shifting my weight.

"I know we ain't been on the best of terms," he begins with, "but, Pan's beard, Teacup, why in the world would you house that soldier-priest? Pan knows he's got the entire assassins' guild after him. You'd be safer thieving in a leper colony!" Petri laughs. His laugh is about as endearing as his jokes.

I scowl. "I'm an acquisitioner, not a thief." The two are different. Sort of. "And Magnus is a friend."

"A friend?" Petri scowls back. "You hadna' met him 'fore tonight. He nearly cost me my job. Barkus lost a lot of money tonight and he ain't happy. And the boys on Dockside ain't too happy, either."

"I told you not to mess around with the Docksiders," I remind him. "Especially not Frank,

Petri grimaces. "Golden-head ain't gonna be 'round fo' never."

I had suspected Barkus was getting a cut of Petri's winnings. It made sense, since Barkus ran the game. But mixing it up with the Docksiders? Barkus looks like a puppy compared to those guys.

"We've got to stick together, us. Come on now. How much of the prize money did Lucinda give pretty-boy anyways? Half? A Third? A peck on the cheek? A—?" He makes an obscene gesture.

My face is hot. Even Lucinda has more class than that.

"I don't have a clue."

It's one thing to take the rough side of Petri's tongue when you've had a decent haul and you've taken it to his darkroom to do business, and quite another to get it on your front doorstep with no mental preparation. I'm on perilous footing.

There is something off about him, too. I can see that. He's standing a little straighter, but in the shadow with a hood over his face, even though it hasn't been raining for an hour or two.

Petri is looking around furtively, like he's already attracted too much attention. Maybe he's just nervous about being away from his post at the Black Cat, but maybe not.

"Mind if I come in?"

I do. I've got three innocents upstairs I don't want exposed. "I'll come down to the Black Cat tomorrow morning. I'm tired."

"Can't wait." He shifts his weight. "Sanjuste needs a retrieval by tomorrow evening, and you're the only one I trust to do it."

"Sanjuste?" The proposal splashes over me like a barrel of herring, and not the preserved kind.

Most of Petri's commissions make me feel a little slimy, even when they aren't followed by the name that tried to put Sara and me out of business by sending thugs to loom over our customers. Thugs. As if Sanjuste isn't bad enough!

He's a great, big bear of a man, but not at all like Magnus. Where Magnus has form and feature, a physique worth sculpting, Sanjuste could be rough-hewn in seven strokes from a single cube of granite. Staring at him, the first thing that hits you (besides his fist) is the never-quite-

17

shaved blood-red stubble on his chin. It's darker than Carmen's hair by a few shades and doesn't make one think of her at all. Bearded, his head is mostly bereft of hair, and his arms and legs are tree trunks, and when he smiles there is nothing but cruelty left. He's a cobbler, but only in the loosest sense. People buy boots from him because there aren't any other options in Lower Ector.

"I told you not to mix with those guys," I repeat angrily, readying to close the door.

"Wait!" Petri's voice sounds a little hoarse. "They're coming after you, Teacup. They'll kill you. And me. They don't care."

"All the more reason to steer clear. I wouldn't touch a job from that murderous bastard with a polearm," I say without thinking. "I don't open the Sara's shop, and his goons leave me alone. That's all I need from him."

Petri's panting hard, like he does when he's angry or scared, which isn't often. "What am I going to do?" he mutters. I almost feel sorry for him. He must have lost a lot of money tonight.

"Listen, Petri. I'll come find you tomorrow morning. We'll figure something out."

His face jumps to his usual scowl. "Good luck finding me, and thanks for nothing." There's a sudden rustling on the other side of the door and now I'm staring into the misty night.

"I'll see you later, Petri."

No response.

I go back upstairs wondering if I should make good on my promise. I have nothing to fence, nor any desire to do a job for Sanjuste. He's a ready fit for the Nightshades if I ever saw one, though perhaps not subtle enough. And I doubt I can do anything to help Petri if he's taken on a bad debt.I'm flat broke. He'll be better off talking to Barkus.

Tracing the wooden beams and the plaster walls helps me shake off the feeling of being violated. The plaster needs a fresh coat, but will easily keep the cold of the looming winter out. My hands relax slowly and my tired bones are barely to the top of the stairs when I hear another knocking, this time soft and timid.

knock.

knock.

knock.

A familiar voice, pleading. "Teamus? Teamus?"

Carmen. Red, curly hair wild, matted with streaks of black. Her petite shoulders and green blouse are ash-stained and nearly defeated. My heart thumps big and sad

19

when I see her soot-stained face, upset for forgetting that it's her shop that burned to the ground tonight. She's about to collapse from exhaustion.

"Teamus. I know you're busy with that dart hero and all, but do you mind if I grab a bit of rug here tonight? The shop's a steaming heap, and I don't know what else to do."

She's got a stiff upper lip but I can tell she's hurting, and that makes me ache even more. That shop meant everything to her.

"Don't even ask."

I make room in the narrow stairwell up to the flat, listening to the swish of her soot-caked petticoat. "Not much to eat, though."

She's too tired to smile, can't seem to keep her chin up.

I shepherd her into the kitchen and refill the wooden wash basin after dumping the cloudy water out the window. She's asleep at the table before washing half her sooty face. I take the washcloth from her limp hand, glad she feels safe here.

Knock. Knock.

"Pan's beard."

Knock. Knock. KNOCK!

It's not a joke. It's Lucinda. She's got an armful of

20

fresh linen for . . bandages? She doesn't wait for an invitation but pushes her way in and up the stairs.

I can hear the clink of a heavy purse—about the right amount of heavy—as she takes the stairs two at a time.

I chase her up to the kitchen, where my last candle is burning to a quick finish. "Lucinda, it's a little too late to. . . ."

Lucinda takes one look at Carmen and winks at me. "Busy night, Teacup?"

"You've no idea." I put a finger to my lips. "Can't you see she's sleeping?"

Lucinda peers around, changing subjects. "Thought you might need some help with Magnus."

"He's asleep, too. You can come back in the morning."

Lucinda pulls a sour face. "I'd rather stay here. There's still a pretty wild party going on down there, and you might need help with Magnus."

"Uh, okay."

I'm too tired to argue, and she might be right. I certainly don't have the energy to do any more for him tonight. I have the vague feeling Magnus might be uncomfortable with her sleeping under the same roof, and not because she's a pickpocket, but it won't matter for tonight. He's sleeping like a dead man.

"You'll have to sleep in the kitchen with Carmen," is the best my tired brain can come up with.

"But then where will you sleep?" Her eyebrow jumps teasingly.

I'm too tired to be teased. "In the attic."

"Why don't you take Carmen with you? I'm sure she'd be more comfortable up there."

I'm pretty sure she wouldn't.

"She's comfortable. Listen, you sure you want to help with Magnus? 'Cause I'll bet that Barkus has quite a mess to clean up tonight and could probably use your help even more than I do!"

Lucinda pipes down. She's feisty, but she knows when to shut it. "You have a spare blanket?"

"You'll have to share with Carmen."

I get them my spare and we hoist Carmen out of her chair and onto the soft rug. Lucinda is more gentle than I've seen her, except maybe when she's feeding the orphans out behind the Black Cat. It isn't but a moment and her golden hair is mixing on the kitchen floor with Carmen's red, and both are sleeping. Carmen's light, soft inhalation is masked by Lucinda's deeper, huskier tone.

Finally.

My aching bones tell me what to do. I'm halfway asleep when there's a sound at the door.

Knock. Knock.

POUND.

POUND. POUND. POUND.

"Youhoooo! Yooohoo? Mishter Shteeps?"

There's a ruckus outside and the clattering of shutters from the third apartment up, just across the narrow alley. The elderly lady that lives there isn't always in the best overall health, but she's got a great set of pipes, some healthy arms, and she doesn't like being woken up.

"PAN'S MANGY BEARD! THIS SHOULD SOBER YOU UP, YOU NOISY SON OF A RAT'S NUT!"

Splash.

"Arrsh!"

I stumble down the stairs, wondering what poor creature got blasted with Sonya Marconey's wastewater. It's Markel, incredibly drunk, but otherwise dry as a brick from the oven.

Where his shirt and coat are, Pan only knows.

"Hi!" His face implies he needs some hospitality.

"Sorry, Markel. No alcohol policy, remember." That's mostly true. I certainly don't drink it, but sometimes I steal

23

it. Nobody really *needs* high quality alcohol, so I don't feel as guilty about fetching it down to Petri for the resale. Some of Barkus's finest drinks come courtesy of my careful wine cellar investigations.

Markel doesn't need to know this though, and his grinning face falls a bit when he realizes that even in the wake of Magnus's stunning victory, I still want him to be sober around my kids. He bounces back quick, though. "Ish he up thersh? The champignon?"

I can't help but smile. Markel makes me laugh. "Yes. Sleeping. Which is where I need to be."

"Wait." Markel scowls. "Ish Lushinda up there?"

I don't bother to answer that one. There's no telling what Markel will do if he finds that out. "Good night, Markel. Goodnight!"

"I'll shtand guard!" he offers, swaying unsteadily as he lowers himself slowly, using the doorframe to help manage his awkward descent. Evidently he's not actually planning to 'stand' guard.

"Never shleep a wink!"

"Not a wink," I insist, closing the door slowly, careful not to pinch his sagging body.

I'm just settling into my knothole in the attic when I remember the bare cupboards, but it doesn't matter: the

24

haze of sleep is already coming. The guests can fend for themselves. "There's only so much you can do, Tee," I remind myself.

There's another knock at the door but my bones are too heavy to investigate whether it's just my imagination or someone really out there banging on the door. Instead, I float away on a puff of cloud, to the tune of more yelling. "Mishter Shteeps shaid, 'No more vishitors tonight!'"

Indistinct noises.

"Unhand thish porsh, fiend!"

Then, more splashing.

Sleep. . .

He lunges at me, midnight cloak billowing. I can feel his long, white claws around my throat. "You've got to tell him, Teacup."

"Tell him what?"

He doesn't answer the question. "I'm dead. Ashfire and starlight." His pallid face smiles crookedly, as sunlight shines on green grass. Light and dark swirl around his face.

I can't quite recognize who I'm talking to. His face is familiar, but only in the dream sort of way, when a face says it's someone that it doesn't really look like.

I remember this face being scarier in the waking world.

"You've got to tell him."

"Who? What?" I say, confused.

"I can't remember, worm-brain. I'm dead." He pauses, rubbing cold, murderous fingertips together. "Have you tried cataloguing all the people you've deceived?"

"Have you tried cataloguing all the times you were 'dead?'"

A raspy, percussive chuckle. "I am though, right?"

I wake—it seems like minutes—to a smell this house hasn't known in years. It's salty and smoky and sweet, and my stomach punches me out of bed so fast I nearly bang my head.

Bacon.

"Sara?"

Sleep clears, and I know it's not her. It's got to be Lucinda. Or Carmen.

I scamper down my ladder—a red-and-gold silk banner that I "borrowed" a few years ago from one of the lookout towers on the southern wall. (I know they have extras, and I can always take this one back, if they run out.) I don't peek over the dividing wall between the closet, bedroom, and the kitchen. I drop straight to the bedroom floor and go through the door.

When I enter, I can see that it's just Timmy and Magnus. Like the rest of the living quarters, the kitchen's on the second floor. Sara and I paid a double handful when we bought this place, just to have the all the space downstairs for inventory and display. And a second story fireplace. *Happy Soles*, we'd called it. We were young and naïve.

Magnus and Timmy have fished out the cast-iron and

27

they're frying bacon. Or rather, Timmy's frying bacon and Magnus is sitting at the long table, directing him in the finer points.

" . . . get too hot. Then the bacon bubbles and sticks to the pan." Even sitting, Magnus is still taller than Timnus, who is small and tidy, like myself.

This morning Timnus is also impatient and hungry, probably salivating. I can tell by the twitchy movements of his short, knobby limbs as he pushes the bacon with the spatula. Normally, he has perfect control. I've caught him playing with Sara's tools before, making little doll outfits for younger kids in the neighborhood. I don't know where he's been getting the leather though. . . and he won't ever let me get a good look. For a 13-year-old, he's surprisingly good at hiding things.

But we're also different. He's definitely less interested in high places than I am. He'd be a good climber, but he prefers to make things with his hands, rather than climb with them.

Timnus starts pulling the bacon out of the pan.

"Not yet, good sir," Magnus laughs. He can't see very well yet—that's odd—but he's sniffing the air. "Give it another minute or two for that fat to render."

Timmy bobs his short, brown hair without saying

anything. He normally doesn't talk, unless there's a purpose in it. Saves room for Val, I think.

Speaking of Val, there's a banging up the staircase, the thumping she makes whenever she's carrying a heavy load of some sort. She enters with an armload of Pan-knows-what. Food, probably. She's followed by a mountain of textile. It's Carmen, carrying enough cloth to bury herself.

"Err."

"Hi, Tee!" she says, blushing slightly. "Sleep okay?" Her angular eyebrows arch imploringly. "I can still make my commission if I hurry."

"There's probably room on the bed," I say, looking at the pile, which is dominated by blues and yellows. I can't help blushing back. There's a tradition in Ector: you've got to be careful just how much hospitality you show a woman.

"Don't worry," she says, guessing my thoughts, "it's just for a couple of days."

"Not worried," I worry quietly.

She lays the cloth on the corner of the bed in the next room, which I notice has been beautifully made.

Suddenly, I'm conscious that my hair doesn't lie flat in the back when I press it down.

There's a snort from behind. Lucinda. I turn just in

29

time to see her approach Magnus, soft-handing him his game-winnings from last night. That's a first, her returning a *full* purse.

"Didn't even make a dent," she says.

"We will see about that," Magnus says, fumbling with the knot to his belt. "Wait till we find those orphans you were talking about."

Lucinda shoots an irritated look at me, one that says I flubbed the dosing. It's my fault he's blind, after all, even if I did save his life. Twice. But that doesn't stop Lucinda from being snippy.

She reaches down to help his fingers finish. "Nonsense, Magnus. If you go throwing money around this side of town you'll attract the wrong sort of attention."

"I want to help them."

"They just need a warm place to stay at night. . . ."

"Not here!" I interrupt. "Even the front porch is taken!"

Valery is setting out plates, short, brown hair fluffing out to the sides where's she's slept on it. She's got beautiful brown eyes and a long face—none of my kin will ever be plump—but her legs and face promise she'll tower over both Timnus and me when she's done growing.

Carmen's crafty fingers have cut some apples, nothing

wasted. It's as if the apple saw her coming and surrendered stem, seeds, and blossom stubble without a fight. She's smiling at the kids, at Lucinda, at me as she passes the slices around. It's the best thing I've tasted in months, including last night's meal from Barkus's kitchen.

"Thanks, Carmen."

"Anytime, Teacup," she says by way of invitation.

Lucinda rolls her eyes.

Valery's head pops up from examining a spot on a faded wooden plate. "Da, there's someone thumping the door below. . . . Want me to check?"

My fingers tingle, slightly hot.

"Nah. Help Carmen." I head for the stairs.

"You sure get a lot of visitors," Magnus offers.

Timnus looks at him with a big grin that reminds me of brown-haired Sara. "Usually only during tax season." I motion for Timnus to shush, but Valery picks up right where Timmy leaves off.

"Last year we got over 14 summons!" she says gleefully. "I counted them."

Magnus looks confused. "In Solange you'd only get two! Then they send the . . ."

"We do things a little differently here in Ector," I call back, already halfway down the stairs.

31

It's too soon for tax collectors, and I've already paid my burden for the year. Or rather, Barkus has, and I've repaid him by drugging Magnus, which I plan to never do again.

Who could it be this time?

I open the door, wondering if Pale Tom's death-spell might have cursed my doorstep. I like peace and quiet and this is getting to be outrageous.

"Teamus Steeps?"

I'm greeted by a broad grin that doesn't quite reach the slanty eyes on his not-tax-collector face. He's got a long, blond braid poking out from beneath the hood, and a pointy ear. His hands are gloved, and his autumn brown clothes are a little too nice for this side of town, a little *too* quiet.

"Who?" I lie. It's my de facto response to questionable inquiries.

He ignores my ploy. He knows it's me. "I have a message on behalf of Tom Leblanc of Maudark."

"Tom's dead," I say trying to push the door shut. "Died last night."

"I know," says the sharp-eared man, smiling broadly, boot smashing into the door and throwing me back. "You did a number on him, I hear. That's why this message is for you."

Time slows like a foggy night. Not like last night, sharp and uniform, when I could see the Nightshades crumbling before a master of their craft, but jerky and in fits and starts, as though from a distance. But still it's slow enough, slow enough to see a blade being drawn from beneath the cloak, and that is something I don't want to happen.

And I know what to do. I've seen Tom do this very thing, one particularly dirty night in the alley, when I happened to catch him working while casing a house from the rooftops. It may not have been as much an accident as I'd previously thought, I realize.

I don't fall back; I fall towards him, my palm hammering the nerve that controls bicep muscles needed for drawing a dagger in reverse grip. My other hand jams down on the pommel pinning his suddenly limp hand in place and pushing the blade back through fabric and flesh. His eyes go wide with pain, but his head descends and I'm not quick enough to get out of the way.

Smash!

Stars. I'm falling now. I catch his braid, and sort of swing on it as I go down. There's a bit of a cracking sound as his head connects with the cool, stone threshold. I flinch as the probably-poisoned-blade in his leg cuts my cheek in passing, but I wiggle out the back between his legs, rolling past rhododendrons in broken pots, up and running before I realize he isn't moving. Blood is dribbling to my shoulder and I'm suddenly worried about passing out.

I wander back towards my house as people scatter. Lower Ector doesn't mind a good brawl, but they'll run for cover if blades are drawn.

I feel dizzy.

"Magnus?" I yell. "Lucinda?"

I don't want the kids to see. Or Carmen.

"Markel?"

No Markel. He's too smart a drunk to be mixed in with this sort of trouble.

I can feel my ability to prioritize fading. I sit down in the doorway, beneath the lintel, right next to the corpse, which I realize isn't a corpse. The man's still breathing, but he's shaking and I can feel the heat radiating from his bare skin. I should probably be doing *something*, but the best I can think of is stealing the pretty black ring he's wearing before someone untrustworthy finds it. Seems important.

His hand is limp, and it's a cinch to twist it off and slip it on my big toe.

Heh Heh! Fits quite well.

For a moment, things come into focus. Tom *wanted* me to have his ring. Not this one. The one I left at the Black Cat last night. He put it deliberately in the false-bottomed jewelry box in that house on Lantern street. The rings are important, but I don't know why.

Headache.

I put a hand to my cheek and more blood—gummy—seeps between my fingers. The sun dims.

What was I doing?

"Magnus?" I croak. I'm too dizzy to get to my feet.

Suddenly, large hands scoop me up. "Teacup. What happened?"

I smell him. It's the smell of strength and fresh bandages. He's carrying me up the stairs quickly, steadily, like I'm no effort at all.

"Message from Tom." I can't manage much else.

Magnus grunts.

There are cries of alarm in the kitchen as the dishing and scooping of food stops. I feel the heat of the crowd around me.

"Give him some space," Magnus says. "Timnus, go halfway downstairs and be my eyes. Yell if anyone approaches. Do not close the door. Do *not* leave the house.

35

Valery, window. Look for men on rooftops. Lucinda,
water. Needle. Thread. Carmanthum. Carmen . . ."

I worry. I don't have much carmanthum; I used most
of it on Magnus last night. I worry about Carmen and the
kids seeing this. About Timnus on the stairs. But my
tongue's not working correctly. My whole face feels numb,
like it's going to sleep.

Valery says something about Petri watching the door,
two roofs over.

How does Petri get on a roof?

In a moment that lasts forever, Timnus is back
reporting, breathless and scared. It doesn't make sense to
me, but it's clear that the not-dead man is now dead,
knifed in the back, not my doing.

I hear Carmen's voice interspersed with Magnus,
arguing ferociously until the two come to some mutual
agreement. I imagine the sharp lines of her face softening
as they move together in some purpose my shaking body
can't comprehend.

Val blurts out suddenly that Petri's gone from his post
and he's talking to the worst possible person: Sanjuste.

My scalp prickles and my hands burn. *Sanjuste.* I try to
rise and stumble, hand going to a knife that isn't there.

Lucinda catches me, whispering frantically in my ear

so no one can hear. "They can't get you here, Teacup. They're afraid of Magnus."

I shake my head, trying to talk. " . . . all . . . missing orphans . . ." I'm back in this very room seven years ago, watching Sara slip away, and the pieces fall into place. "Sara," I gasp.

Sanjuste the cobbler. Sanjuste the Cruel. Sanjuste, a man that not even Tom would mentor. . . . And with Ector's chief assassin gone, there's no one to check the man's lust for blood, not even the dark code of the Nightshades.

Lucinda's face goes white with understanding, but *she* keeps her head, puts her hand on my forehead. "Magnus, he feels like a furnace! I need *cold* water."

I can't really see what anyone else is doing, but I know there's a flurry of movement as they clear the oak table and lay me on it.

Lucinda doesn't stop whispering in my ear. "Hang on, Teacup. We'll deal with Sanjuste, but we need you. Your kids need you. Carmen needs you. Magnus and I need you." I don't know if she's speaking truth, but it's nice to hear. I only understand about half the words, my heart tripping like a three-legged dog trying to climb a tree.

The world is burning around me. They're splashing

37

me with water, cutting off my clothes, forcing a wooden spoon between clenching teeth, and I can hear my own head banging against the table. *Thump. Thump. Thump.* Or maybe that's my heart?

Sanjuste. Suddenly, all I can think is how I told Sara not to press him, not to take his clients. Not from a man who'd had spent time in the far south, done boot work in Byzantus. Not from a man who liked watching people suffer. I guess I'd known secretly, even then.

Now I'm the one shaking on the table, just like Sara seven years ago. Nothing anyone does is going to save me.

Him. I try gasping through the wooden spoon, but my jaw is too busy grinding the wood.

Carmen—frightened and determined—is holding my hands, Lucinda my feet, and Magnus my head when I lose consciousness in a cloud of pain and white light.

For a split second, Pale Tom is standing over me, kicking me in the side, a scowl of surprised fury on his face. "Get up, you little runt. Go teach that fat dungwad a lesson. Then you can die. No apprentice of mine will be killed by that grungulous wad of toad shistle . . ."

My world flashes again, bright-white lightning burning through the red-orange fire of hell in my bones. I gasp awake.

38

Huuuaahhh!

I'm not on the table anymore. Magnus is holding me over his knee, my head down, my feet in the air, probably trying to keep as much of the poison out of my bloodstream as possible. Been a long time since I've been upside-down over someone's knee. I keep waiting for the spanking.

Timmy is crying softly, promising to never lift another thing in his whole life, or spy on the neighbor's daughter drying her wash, if Pan will just let his Da live.

Magnus says three words, his voice strangely feeble. "It's not your fault, Timnus."

Or five. I can't concentrate.

"I've seen true evil now, Jeremiah." Magnus whispers.

I can't move my head. Magnus's beefy arms have me clamped up tight, and he's pinching the skin on my face till it oozes, the yellowish blood dripping from my cheek onto the floor. I can see it pooling next to Magnus's gigantic bare foot and neatly trimmed toenails.

I fade in and out as he massages my face like a baker kneading dough.

Darkness.

Ow.

Darkness.

Ow-ww.

Eventually the room stops shaking, Lucinda stops splashing my face, and I realize that it's confessional time for Valery. I'm upright now, Carmen pricking my face like I'm one of her embroidered dresses. It doesn't hurt as she tugs the thread, not like it should.

"Oh, Da. We never should have done it." Val says. She's holding me steady in the chair, being my spine. It feels like every muscle in my body has gone limp.

I should be focusing on her, saying something to calm her down, but I'm not. My mind is racing. Some poisons kill so fast you'll die if you haven't already taken an equally toxic antidote.

"Lordmort," a voice in my head says. In my mind's eye, I'm perched on the crossbeam of the Black Cat. Below me, Pale Tom is unusually talkative, telling stories of poison and soaking up shadows from his usual corner. Carmen's at the bar, listening, not drinking.

Prick.

Pull.

Prick.

"Lordmort," Carmen says out loud as she stitches.

Quiet muttering in the house.

I should be dead.

40

Valery trembles, but holds me upright.

When Carmen pauses, I glance over at Magnus. He's bent over the washbasin, vomiting. Lucinda has her arm roped around him, holding him steady.

He straightens. ". . . okay now. Thanks. Never had to take that much before."

Lucinda dumps the basin out the window, rinses it with water from the bucket, and dumps it again.

"Timmy, I'll watch the door for a bit," Magnus says. His face pallid; he fixes his eye on something in the distance and mutters, "Watch the rooftops."

Val starts talking again. "Oh, Da! We didn't mean to cause trouble!"

"What are you talking about, Val?" My voice comes out in a whisper. I feel shaky, like I've just chased a runaway cart down the hill.

"It's our fault they're out to get you," she says.

"It's not . . ."

"Timnus got caught spying on Master Sanjuste again."

"Caught?" I mumble. "If he'd caught you, you wouldn't be here blurting out your secrets." Or, that's what I try to say.

She understands. "I didn't mean 'catch'," she blushes. "I meant 'saw.' We were spying on him and he saw us."

41

Why Timnus would want to case another cobbler's shop is beyond me. We have all the same tools downstairs, and better quality. If he had anything worth stealing, I'd have taken it ages ago as payback for driving us to work so hard. But now I have two more reasons to hate him: Sarah's "fever" and my own.

"Val. I've told you Sanjuste isn't safe. He's a thug."

"But Timmy made me shoes!" she says. "He just needed to know how to tie off the stitch."

My eyes travel down her narrow face and brownish hair, her skinny waist, and her too-long legs shooting to the floor.

Not shoes, but riding boots. They're made of fine, solid leather, dark red, set together so well that I can't see a stitch. They aren't perfect. The cuts aren't high-precision, and the leather gathers in several places where it shouldn't, but they look functional and stylish, definitely not what I would call a waste of good leather.

"Wow," I say. "Timmy made those boots?" I realize I'm discussing shoes with my beautiful daughter while my face is being stitched up. It hurts to smile.

"Yes," she says, blushing. "Don't be mad. You're going to be okay. Everything is okay, right?"

She looks at me with the hope of a naïve thirteen-year-old.

"We'll make it," I say, masking my worry.

She smiles, and starts bouncing in her new red boots. She's as talkative as Timnus is quiet. "I know you don't like us messing around in the shop. But we were careful to put all the tools back so you wouldn't notice, and . . ." She realizes what she's just admitted to and pales. "Oops."

"I'm not mad." Instead I feel unreasonably happy. The boots aren't something I'd have sold to our upper-row customers, but they would pay for themselves, labor and a bit to spare, if sold fair market. "Actually this is great! You two can pay the taxes on this place next year!"

"Da-a!"

Lucinda is watching Val fondly, hands momentarily idle. I risk a glance at Carmen. Her look of concentration is betrayed by the tiny wrinkles of a smile around her eyes. I'd thrill at the touch of her fingers on my face, except she happens to be poking me with a sharp, sharp needle.

"Where did Timmy get the plans?" I ask, wiggling my toes. 'How' might have been a better question. I already recognize the design. It was Sara's favorite riding boot for women. Timmy didn't just steal Master Sanjuste's craft; he's been flipping through Sara's secret trade book. A book locked inside a chest inside a chest under the

43

millstone beneath floor planks.

"Mom's book."

"You mean the one locked in a double-chest and buried in the foundation?"

This time she blushes more deeply. "I . . . I helped Timmy unlock it."

I smile to show her it's okay. "Just don't let Sanjuste see you wearing those."

"About Sanjuste," Lucinda says. "I think avoiding him isn't the best plan. I . . . ." She trails off suddenly, realizing Timnus and Magnus aren't in the room.

"Lucinda," I say, suddenly worried. "Where's Magnus?"

"He asked Timmy to . . ."

Her face goes white as she realizes the hunk of twisted metal that was by the fireplace is now missing. A hunk of metal that used to be a sword.

She's down the creaky stairs in an instant, with me stumbling after, hot on her trail, and Carmen and Val chasing both of us.

"Teamus! *Stop*! I haven't tied you off yet!"

I stop.

"Val, come back!"

But she's in close pursuit of Lucinda, boots churning.

Clompityclompclompclompclompity.

Timnus still needs a few pointers on sizing, it seems.

"Teamus, wait!" Carmen catches me beneath the lintel, reaches up, and ties off the stitching in one deft and angry motion. "I'm. Not. Done."

"Ow!"

I look around. "Where is the body?"

Her face is worried and her jaw is set. "Magnus reported it to the authorities. Someone sent the corpse-bearers while you were unconscious."

"They ask for a statement?"

"No. They'd heard about your little riot last night and thought the man was hoping to cash in on your winnings."

I shake my head. "It was a Nightshade. They've got it in for Magnus, and now they've got it in for me."

"Don't say that, Tea."

"You weren't there last night, not when the dark guild showed up."

"And I'm glad. I was working on a blouse that I'll have to remake from scratch. As far as I'm concerned, there's only one Nightshade in Ector, and he likes you. I've heard him say it."

"When." My heart thumps.

"Last week. Over a friendly game."

45

I swallow hard. "Tom's dead."

Carmen looks surprised, puts a hand to her mouth. More proof that Pale Tom was an odd fellow, even for a Nightshade. Carmen can keep her head down, but she doesn't approve of violence, let alone murderers.

I get back to the point. "Tom wasn't the only Nightshade in town," I insist. I show her the ring pulled from my would-be assassin.

"A ring."

"It's called an Oath. A Nightshade's Oath. You can see the smoke actually moving on its black edges."

"Put it away, Teacup," she mutters. "Or throw it into the river. I've lost more than a dress shop to those murderers." She wraps her nimble fingers around my wrist and pushes my hand toward my thin pockets. "I can't stand to think of losing you. Or of you killing anyone, even a Nightshade."

"I didn't kill him," I say, slipping the ring into my pocket. "He was still alive when Magnus found me."

"How did you get the ring, then?"

"He accidently poisoned himself while trying to stab me. After that it was pretty easy. Lordmort is deadly."

"Can we go upstairs and talk about something else?"

"I want to find my kids."

Carmen sighs. She's worried about me being up and about but can see that I won't be nursed right now. "Okay. But you should lock your door."

I lock the door to the apartment staircase. *Where is Magnus?*

We're walking now. She's still holding my wrist, so I take her hand—cold as ice—and warm it up. She doesn't let go.

One block passes, all brown beams and white plaster, a few passers-by, and a butcher's stall, not the freshest.

Two blocks. The tension between us lessens, even though she pushes me down on a raised doorstep to help me catch my breath.

I scan the lane for any useful sign, following Carmen's eyes to the center of a brown- speckled stone fountain in the middle of the square. I'm not sure why it's running— perhaps because the cistern on the keep-wall is overfull— but the big bowl is loaded up with water and two young children are playing in the thin flow while shopping parents have their backs turned.

The kids are soaked to their knees, as if last night wasn't wet enough, and the gray clouds above aren't threatening still more. Somewhere in their minds, it is still summer.

47

The little girl splashes the little boy. "Chase me, chase me!" she chants. She has a short, blond mane—almost white—and rosy cheeks.

At first he doesn't seem to notice. He's kicking water and pretending to protect her, swinging his puny arms like a dragon-warrior.

"Hector!" She splashes him, this time on his dry, white tunic where he's sure to notice it.

"What?"

"You've already *killed* that dragon." Rosy-Cheeks smiles. "I'm safe now, silly."

"Oh." There's a brief pause as he thinks up an excuse. "But then there's *another* dragon! I have to fight it, too!" he growls, raising his sword arm above soaked linen, preparing for a truly epic battle.

"Hector! Come here! I have a surprise."

Hector lets out an exasperated breath but splashes over to her, stopping just out of hug's reach.

"Close your eyes."

"I'm not closing my eyes," he says suspiciously. Then he realizes this might offend her. "The dragon might eat me."

"Do it." Rosy insists, imperiously.

Hector obeys this time, but I can tell he's peeking.

48

Rosy steps close, pressing an imaginary something into Hector's hand and he looks confused.

"It's a ring," she clarifies. "You took good care of me."

"Oh." Hector's face is solemn. "I will always be worthy of it."

I don't think he understands these traditional words, but Carmen does. She's still looking over her shoulder as we leave Fountain Square.

I make sure she has enough leverage to see by letting go of her now-warm hand.

"Did you ever want that sort of ring?" she asks me guardedly.

"Huh?" I pretend not to have heard, buying think-time, standing to get us moving again, though it is painful.

"The good kind. The committing kind."

She hums half of a tune while I think.

"Once. Maybe twice." I catch up a dropped flower from the cobblestone and dry it off for her, just for luck. It doesn't match her hair or her dress, but she smiles anyway.

We wander for a bit. I relax about my kids. They're with two people that I've learned to trust deeply in the last twenty-four hours, the closest thing I've got to friends, besides Carmen. We keep looking though, just in case.

Halfway across the river, on the mid-island greenspace, old men are tossing rings, the large brass kind, at horse stakes sticking out of the ground. They're singing snatches of old drinking songs, scratching parts that shouldn't be scratched in public, and glancing furtively at the women gathered in the shade of the tailor's pavilion to gossip. Everyone is taking advantage of this last bit of soft, gray weather before the cold.

The brass sings too, clinking metallically when each ring hits another.

After just two blocks west along the waterfront, I realize I'm not going to make it through upper Ector. The stitches are hot and painful on my face. "I don't think I'm going to make it much farther."

"It will be okay, Teacup." Carmen puts her hand on my arm consolingly. "That big fellow seems to know what he's doing."

"Magnus."

"Magnus," she agrees. "And Lucinda will look after

Val. You need to rest. You're already pushing your luck. Right."

"Let's head back."

I follow her lead, but I'm not stepping lightly. I'm plodding. Heavy.

We take the Lantern Street Bridge. Carmen looks around, gray eyes taking in everything. I keep my head down and ignore the dark grinning window-eyes of one particular house.

Soon I realize we're almost home, also not far from the Black Cat. I point down the road. "I want to see your shop in daylight."

Her red curls shake in negation. "Waste of time."

"I still want to see it."

She gives in. She knows I can see things that other people miss. The wooden wreckage is still smoldering, and last night's rain left muddy ash rivers in the cobblestone crevices. The wall adjacent to the Black Cat is completely burned out, along with the front corner of the shop and part of the roof immediately above it. The remaining roof is sagging. Huge chunks of the wall are missing on every side, where axe crews hacked their way in to douse the interior. Everything has taken on a greenish cast where the smoke gathered and permeated the stack.

Seeing the carnage gives me strength to push myself. I help Carmen recover a few more bits of hardware, including her favorite thimble, and we discuss the futility of washing the fabric inventory. Who wants a smoke-scented shirt? But we might be able to do something else with the putrid cloth.

"Can we hang it on a line over night?"

"We can try." I'm not optimistic, but we gather up the best of it and drape it over the Black Cat's horse post.

Creeping around in the wreckage, I get angry, thinking about the little people smashed to pieces in Ector. Carmen's shop, my family, stability. There's a disease here, and it's us. Tom and his cronies. Men like Sanjuste. Even Barkus, extorting orphans in exchange for leftover food.

It hits hard, like this morning's poison. Or maybe this shaking is an aftershock? I don't care. Someone tried to kill me today. In front of my kids. I may be small, but if I'm going down, I'm taking big people with me, and not the ones I love.

Crossing cobblestone, I nip into the Black Cat while Carmen takes another turn through the fallen timbers.

Actually, I pick the lock and slip the bar, which are no match for me. I'd go through the hole in the wall but it's already been boarded up.

My eyes adjust to the gloom immediately, fast even by my standards. The first thing I notice? The Reigning Champion plaque has been taken down. In its place is last night's dart board with Magnus's winning throw wedged into the metal and Grippy's flanking throws still standing to either side of it.

I slip on my new black ring from this morning and things come into focus for me. I feel angry. And quick. I also feel an unnatural urge to smile and shudder.

I take the ring off, though it clings to my finger slightly. Too small.

Calm. Slow.

Put the ring back on.

Smoldering. Strong. Smiling.

Then there is shuffling from the kitchen. "Tamara? Is that you?"

Barkus sees my not-Tamara shape.

"Front of the house is closed for another hour. I can call the town guards if you need a second opinion."

I'm not turning tail now. I leap to the top of the polished chestnut bar, where Petri normally minds his bookie box. It's a chest-high jump, from a flat-footed stance, but I land it easily, though it shakes something loose in my stomach. "I've got my own opinions, thank you," I say softly.

I do my best menacing crouch on the bar, with my hand over my face, trying not to vomit from the sudden movement. My fingertips push into the woodgrain, centering me.

Barkus sucks in a breath. A shadowy figure crouching on your closed bar isn't the start of a comedy. His face is white as a sheet, and he turns to run back into the kitchen.

"You move and I'll put my dagger through your ear."

It's a bluff, but he's not taking any chances. He freezes.

I slink down the bar toward him, still trying not to throw up.

"Petri tried to hire me for a job late last night. What was it?"

"Teacup? I don't know anything," he begs. He keeps his eyes averted, submissive.

That's a first.

"Where is Petri?" I ask.

"I . . . I don't know."

"No. I don't suppose he'd stick around once he's pissed off a Nightshade." I let that bit sink in, let him see my new ring from the corner of his eye. All things considered, I like the one that I got from Pale Tom better.

This one has a sour, crazy taste to it. I can't wait to take it off and throw it down the nearest well.

"What *do* you know, Barkus? I don't have a lot of time." Or the extended skill set. Or the inclination. But he doesn't know this. I take out my knife and inspect its edges in the gloom, copying something I'd seen others do.

It seems pretty effective because Barkus starts talking immediately. "Sanjuste rolled in last night about the time we started sending people home, said he was looking for Petri." Barkus is sweating now, and it smells like onions. I guess he's not as tough as he looks.

"I thought Sanjuste didn't come around here," I growl.

"He must have heard about Tom."

 I think about that.

"Why was he afraid of Tom, Barkus?"

"Everyone was. . . ."

"Don't waste my time." I twitch my knife in the air a bit and he flinches.

"Tom nearly slit his throat once for offering to do a bit of side-work. Please, Teacup. I'm not supposed to know that."

Outside I can hear Carmen calling for me. "Teacup?"

Time's up.

Barkus is staring at my ring.

I follow his gaze. "Yes. I am." This is not strictly true: I haven't taken any oaths. "Tell that bastard Petri if he—or any other thug, bookie, cobbler, or Nightshade—ever shows a face on Redemption Alley again, I'll make them wish Master Tom was back in business." I do my best impression of a Pale Tom sneer and strut to the door, adding at the last minute, "And if anyone even dreams of touching my kids or my friends, we're going to have a little Pale Tom Party—one the world has yet to see!"

Barkus fidgets but doesn't say anything. He just nods, and his eyes flit to the cellar door, betraying a soft rustle there. I can see Tamara's eyes peeking out from the crack and I resist the urge to shout "Boo." A day ago, she'd have smiled at me and tried to cheat me out of a queenpence. All in good fun, of course.

"Hi, Tamara," I say instead. "Did you put anything different in that drink you gave Magnus?"

"No."

I can hear her hair swish behind the door as she shakes her head.

"He still can't see well," I say.

"Try Carmanthum."

"We did."

"Sorry, then."

From the way her voice comes through the cellar door, I know she's belly-down on the stone stairs. An odd way to hide.

"That can't be comfortable."

"It's not."

I leave so they can get back to business, and before the craziness of what I've just done sinks in. Impersonate a Nightshade. Threaten the underworld. Send a message to Sanjuste and Petri that I don't mind dancing daggers. I'm a survivor, not a killer, even if surviving means making threats at the right time.

I start shaking on Main and don't stop till I reach Redemption Alley, even with Carmen helping me. From a few doors down, I can see Valery leaning against the side of the house, rolling a stylus between her fingers while Lucinda pounds on my door in frustration.

"Teacup. We know you're up there!" It's twice ironic since I now know that Val could open the door in moments with the stylus she's playing with, but no need for Lucinda to know that.

Carmen giggles and it lightens my load.

"I'm coming, Lucinda. And don't rush me on the stairs. I've had a very bad morning!"

Carmen giggles again, this time joined by Valery, who

has watched our approach till now with a sly little smile.

I smile back at her. I can't help it. I love my kids.

Lucinda stops pounding and spins around sheepishly. "Oh! Teacup! I thought you'd stayed home."

"Nope," I shake my head, remembering how tired I am.

"Did you find Magnus or Timmy?" she asks.

"No."

"They'll turn up," Carmen says, jumping in.

I let Carmen lead me back upstairs and tell me what to do. When she says I need to go take a nap, I follow her directions to the letter, down to the detail of sleeping in a bed I haven't personally used in seven years.

When I wake up, Carmen has a bowl of broth for me, salty, with a bit of chicken in it to flavor the potato and carrot. It's not the most delicious thing I've ever tasted, but it's close. She watches me apprehensively.

"It's good," I reassure her. "Aren't you going to join me?"

Carmen glances over at Lucinda, who is flipping through one of the few books I've managed to hold on to over the years. She's staring at it hungrily while Val explains how I used to read her bedtime stories. "We ate about an hour ago," Carmen says.

"An hour? Plus cook time?"

She nods, and takes the bowl from me when I finish, even though I insist on washing it myself.

"Rest." Her hand pushes me firmly back into my chair.

"Ok."

I can feel Lucinda's eyes on me, and I arch my eyebrow. *What?*

She puts the book down and slides over, subtle as a pickpocket. Nobody else notices.

"How does one properly hold a dagger?" There's a determined look in her eye, the same one that says she won't take no for an answer. "Someone has to protect you

60

two," she says, glancing at Carmen.

"And Magnus?"

She ignores the question. "What do I do?"

"Depends on the kind," I whisper back.

What she shows me is a rusty, double-edged Ralfian with a thin, stubby crossguard and no quillons. It's definitely past its prime but still functional, and only slightly oversized for her hand. Not a bad pick for a beginner.

"Reverse, hammer, forward, and palm-enforced." I flip through the basic grips at my side so no one else is likely to see. "Stick with forward. Only idiots and Nightshades use the palm-enforced, and reverse grip is for stabbing people from behind. Mostly."

"Thanks, Teacup."

"Just don't use the pointy end on me."

She smiles reassuringly, eyes twinkling, and slips it back into her dress pocket. There's a light snapping sound as it clicks into place.

Interesting.

The door bangs open downstairs and another small crowd rolls in. They're arguing and talking, and a surprisingly-lucid Markel is bragging about having once been sober for a whole week.

61

Timmy congratulates him for this incomparable effort. "If you keep that up, maybe Da'll invite you to dinner."

Maybe I should reconsider my rules. I'm no saint, either.

Lucinda is down the stairs in a flash.

"Hullo, Lucinda!"

"Hello, Markel. Nice to see you." A pause. "Magnus. . . ."

I can't make out what she is saying to Magnus but his response is as calm as a summer breeze.

"Lucinda, you have to report these things. The town guard needs to know, or they won't be able to do anything."

"They won't be doing anything anyways, not unless you bribed them."

More footsteps on the stairs.

"Markel, come have dinner."

Markel declines Magnus's invitation. "Promised Teacup I'd guard the door."

"Not a bad idea," Magnus affirms. "We'll send some food down."

They're still bickering as they enter the kitchen. "Timmy said we could trust them," Magnus argues. "Is there anyone honest in Ector?"

I do my best to meet his eyes. "Yes."

He beams at me, but his aim is off again.

Timmy pipes up. "Relax, Lucinda!" His squeaky boy-man voice is full of indignation. "We went to Northgate!"

"You went all the way to Northgate?"

I raise my eyebrows enough to remember Carmen's helpful handiwork on my cheek.

My son's voice drips with sarcasm. "Why do you think we've been gone all day? 'Cause we're slow?"

"What about Captain James?" Val counters. "Remember when he . . ."

Timnus turns on her with a little more deference, but not much. He loves her, but he doesn't love people assuming he hasn't thought something through. Where Val rushes in, Timnus is a thinker, like his mother.

"Val, have *you* seen Captain James lately?"

"No."

"Well, I haven't either. And with all this phlegm what's been flying about, I sure wasn't taking Magnus down to the barracks to look for him."

Val doesn't argue the point. She trusts Timmy's judgment as soon as she realizes he's used it. Like I used to trust Sara's. "Well, you should have at least told us that's what you were doing. Lucinda and I searched all Lower

63

Ector for you!"

Timnus gives her "the look" but says nothing.

Magnus shakes his head in disbelief. "You shouldn't have to walk across the entire city to find a guard you trust."

"I think we're lucky to have *one* we trust," Lucinda mutters.

Dinner is a quiet affair. We've never really thought about things—guards, for example—in Magnus's terms. It's always just been that way. Then Magnus says his eyes are getting cloudier and his headache is coming back. This puts a damper on everyone's spirits, especially mine. It's not supposed to last this long.

The food is good though, and between Magnus and Carmen we have a feast that this house has never seen before. Skillet-cooked potatoes and carrots with garlic and butter. More sliced apples. Thick, brown bread slathered in butter and littered with shelled pumpkin seeds. Fresh milk. Two (small) braised chickens. A hard Dowardian cheese, courtesy of a grateful artisan, who had been—Lucinda discovered—hiding in his cheese basement for the last three weeks on the rumor that Pale Tom had been planning a hit on him. (Lucinda suspects the rumor to be the work of a competitor, but only Magnus complains about the injustice of such tactics. The rest of us are used to these sorts of things.)

The clean-up happens equally fast, in spite of Magnus trying to help, with the twins prompting everyone else on the appropriate cupboard locations. Lucinda commits to doing the early morning shopping. Not just because she likes sleepy pockets. She used to enjoy doing the early market provisioning for Barkus. I wonder who he's going to send in her place. Probably Geller, one of the cooks.

Lucinda takes orders and asserts, "Magnus, you better take control of your purse or I might come back wearing something 'presentable.'"

Magnus blushes. "You don't need to change your outfit to look presentable." Since his walk to uptown, it's evident that he's a little more familiar with what some Ectorian ladies consider 'presentable.' "There is *nothing* wrong with what you're wearing."

"Nothing?" Lucinda teases.

Magnus blushes deeper.

I take my leave because Carmen is looking pointedly at me as if considering the same thing. I can't imagine her in something 'presentable.' Or if I can, I'm not admitting it.

And I am most certainly *not* blushing.

Lucinda whispers something in Carmen's ear as I'm leaving, and Carmen's broad grin shows bright, white teeth.

I lean back around the doorframe to remind everyone of the facts: "Only half of what Lucinda says is true."

"I'll take half," Carmen retorts and Lucinda giggles.

My knot-hole isn't as cozy as I remember it. There's laughter downstairs, and probably more blushing, and talk of taking food down to Markel, who is lounging on the front porch again. I crawl out my secret hatch in the brown wood shingles and peer over the eaves at him. He's come up with a large mug of something strong, but he doesn't seem to be drinking it. Rather, he's sitting upright, scanning the stars and rooftops with intelligent eyes, the most sober I've seen him.

I crawl back into my straw-filled attic platform and smell the faded grass and the bits of cloth I've gathered. It's warm and clean. A safe-smelling place.

I doze.

Pale Tom doesn't wait a second to come and visit me. "Didn't you kill me?" he haunts.

"No."

Pale Tom seems to consider this. "Hmm. I suppose that's good," He says, completely unaware of his hypocrisy, humming a dirge while I wade through a dreamscape of ropes and banners.

"Who killed me?" he snaps eventually.

"Magnus."

"Oh." His voice is surly and he nibbles on a fingernail. "I was hoping to die in rivers of blood."

"You made a decent showing."

"But you must have helped. Did you at least stab, maim, blind, pickpocket, or otherwise exercise power over my ultimate person?"

"I didn't touch you."

"You did. I can feel it here." He point's vaguely to his collar bone.

I shake my head adamantly, until I remember my small blade driving into his collarbone. I feel the warm blood beneath my fingertips.

Tom sees my answer before I say anything. "Of course you did. That's why I picked you."

"For what?"

Tom starts to fade again. "Can't remember."

And I'm back in my bed, sweating from the poison I took this morning.

Now I can't sleep. Below I hear Magnus's relaxed breathing, heavy as he exhales, matched in cadence by the breath of my sleeping twins.

There's a candle in the kitchen. I can hear Lucinda chatting with Carmen, who is still working on a mysterious project that she won't show anyone. They giggle as the bell tolls for the watch change. They weren't joking about staying up late.

I listen in. It's a habit I can't avoid, like eating, breathing, or climbing.

Carmen's talking about different stitches and what they're good for, and why the upper crust are willing to make the trek to Lower Ector to visit her.

Lucinda sounds impatient with this. It isn't a topic that interests her, except in the practical way of getting oneself dressed. She turns the subject to me. "What about Teacup?"

There's a clunk on the table as one of them puts something down. Their voices dip out of range for a little while, but soon they forget. " . . . wouldn't hurt a fly, Carmen. He's smart, but he's also gentle."

"I know he isn't like Brock, Lucinda, but I'm still

afraid. And I don't want to be in Lower Ector for the rest of my life, either. I've worked too hard for that."

"Teacup's portable. You can take him with you. He fits in almost anywhere, and he learns quick. The two of you—the four of you—wouldn't have to stay in Lower Ector. Have you seen the shoes Timmy can make?"

There's a weighted pause.

"I like the kids, too." Carmen's voice.

I start to smile, but my cheek hates me for it.

The conversation turns to Magnus. I can tell because I catch his name, and it sounds like Lucinda is throwing it out there for advice. Their voices are too low to hear, but now Carmen is doing most of the talking, taking the tone of an older, more experienced sister.

And then I hear sighs below, and the scraping of chairs. The candle goes out.

"Thanks, Carmen. I needed that." Lucinda's voice.

Carmen's soft voice couples with the closing of a small fabric trunk: "He'll come around, Lucinda. This is a very different sort of game you're playing. Just be patient."

"I'm not very good at that."

"But you're twice as clever as the rest of us. You'll figure it out."

I wait in bed for sleep to return, but it's flown the coop. I'm still shaking, and think it best to get a bit of exercise. Time to prowl, my body says.

"Ok. Just don't do anything foolish."

I won't, it tells me.

It's probably true. I've always liked sneaking. Sounds say too much about a person. You can hide your soul by sneaking.

I used to sneak into the house and surprise Sara at her workbench when I first took her ring. It was fun the first few times, until she actually swung her mallet at me in fright. I should have saved the surprises for the washbasin, where getting wet is the primary concern.

Some ideas come far too late.

And climbing. Pan's beard, I like climbing. When I was little—not that I ever really got big—I would climb the trees outside the city gates until the branches started bending. I could get higher and faster than any other kid in town. The city guards back then called me "Lookout" because of this, and because of my habit of getting underfoot.

I climb down and then back up my silk banner twice

73

for fun, experimenting with different foot locks and drop rolls on the silk rope. Stalling. Curtain sliding. Swinging. I imagine the remaining poison beading out in my sweat, dripping on the planks below, and my thoughts wander.

What *is* Carmen working on? I would never do anything to hurt her, but it won't hurt to take a little peek, will it?

Peek?

Hah.

The kitchen is pitch black now, but I don't light a candle or anything. I know that Lucinda and Carmen have made up cots, and I know how to avoid them. Carmen's box is on the opposite side of the room from where they're sleeping, under the table.

The thought of knowing what secret thing she's working on fills me with excitement and dread, and I can't say why.

It's probably some dress for the fat Duchess of Rose Row, or for the Lady Sterling, so bony and thin that the children say she has worms. This prospect is disheartening. Carmen can make the finest gowns. Why waste quality work on those sour faces, even if they do have deep pockets? I've seen the way they glide over the masses of Lower Ector.

Take money where you can, I guess.

Maybe this is why I struggle with paying taxes and buying bread. Picking a quality mark is hard. "You're too soft," Lucinda's always telling me. "You could be the richest man in Ector!"

Whatever. I'm not interested in making life harder for those already suffering. Lucinda gets this, even if she won't admit it: more than half of what she steals buys food for the less fortunate.

I decide against peeking, and climb halfway back up my silk banner. It's none of my business what she's working on.

My hands disagree. Quality is always their business. I drop-slip down two-thirds. If I know what it is, I might be able to find a matching accessory, or a complimentary fabric, something to make the perfect effect.

I know I'm rationalizing, but this time I don't bother to stop myself. I ghost down the remaining silk, land quietly and tiptoe—though it's more like a glide—through the master room, and have my hand in the box before I even really know what I'm doing.

What's this?

The cloth is unspeakably soft. It's a fabric I've never felt before, one that seems to carry its own warmth, and I can feel the heat in my hand reflected back from the thin fabric. I've never held anything like it.

The shape of it is familiar—leggings, a little on the small side—and I know for certain they aren't for the Fat Duchess. For one thing, she never wears leggings. For two, I don't think the Fat Duchess has ever been this skinny. In fact, there aren't many people in town these *would* fit. A few kids, perhaps. . . .

I let it go, smoothing it back into its place, knowing I've been cooped up too long, looking for exits in all the wrong places.

Just a little prowl?

No. I need to be here, protecting my family.

And my . . . friends, though the word doesn't quite capture what I feel for Magnus, Lucinda and Carmen.

I sit quietly between Carmen and Lucinda, who is almost as loud asleep as Magnus, and think about the mystery fabric, fascinated. I love quality, loved tracing Sara's masterpieces, memorizing the folds and stitching so I could sell them for her. We were a good team. I could always tell who needed new shoes.

Sanjuste had no chance against the two of us.

My face burns at the thought. He tried to kill me today, even without any clear and present threat. And somehow he poisoned Sara, I'm sure of it now. It wasn't a sudden fever after all. She'd cut herself on one of her tools, just a little prick.

I feel sick inside. Why? Just for a bit of extra business? I'd call for justice, but that sort of prayer falls on deaf ears in Ector.

The clouds clear for moment—driving away thoughts of revenge—and moonlight sprinkles the kitchen in silver. A pleasant breeze tells me Lucinda and Carmen have left the window open. The weather is cool and damp, Lady Autumn getting ready for winter. The air floats fresh, promising more rain than the river Neiss knows what to do with.

My hand brushes against another masterpiece: red hair. I've always wondered but never been brave enough to touch it. The curl is coarse and weighty, as textured and living as I'd imagined. There's a faint smell of charcoal about it still, but not unpleasant.

I have the horrible realization that this would fetch a pretty penny on the black market. My lips snarl at the thought, and I let the last curl unwind from my index finger. That *would* be stealing.

Hypocritical? Not at all. Stealing is when you take something because you can, even if you don't need it.

Acquisitioning is. . . .

Okay, so maybe it's a stretch. But there is a difference between a guy who takes your last meal and a guy who takes what he needs to get by. Lantern Street is a perfect example. The Widow Pétanque left some valuables to her nephew, Nori, when she died . . . a nephew I knew for a fact to be a con.

So I'd planned a job with no cut for anyone else. It would probably set me up for a few months at least, and fake Nori didn't deserve the inheritance. Of course, I didn't know yet that Pale Tom had already moved in.

It's obvious now that Tom had expected me to visit Lantern Street. He'd set me up. And then died. Intentionally. It makes me wonder: was there anything else he meant me to have?

I hear faint laughter in my ears.

Of course. On Lantern Street.

Tom's permanent residence isn't safe, not even for me. It's where the Nightshades will look. But Lantern Street was our little secret. If he left me anything, it'll be there. And if I'm just imagining things, at the very least I can retrieve my bag and a few odds and ends, some odds more valuable than others. . . .

I climb back up to my knot-hole. There's a cutaway in

the wood-shingle roof, the one I used earlier to spy on Markel. It's my secret way in and out of the house. I wiggle out through the hatch and I'm on the rooftops, enjoying the silver moon with a glance, saluting the cool stars, breathing brisk, wet air.

In a second I'm running across the rooftops, flying between buildings. My toes grab hold of the grainy, wooden shingles between my feet, resisting the splinters by virtue of calloused sole.

Pitter-patter.

I know short cuts, places that aren't dead-ends, up here between the shingles and the clouds. I hide behind chimneys when I need to, feeling the rough, warm brick on my ribs as the guards move about below.

Ector has a curfew, but I don't worry about it. There aren't many guards surefooted enough to patrol the rooftops, and their leather armor (if they aren't wearing metal) creaks and rubs like a farmer's horse-cart harness.

When I get to Lantern Street, I hear noise. Someone stooped at the lock.

Fake-nephew Nori, out in the plain.

I laugh to myself. Pale Tom didn't even bother to trap that door. He bolted it to the stone. It doesn't even open anymore. Nori's going to be there for a long time, beating his head against a door just as fake as he is.

I take the high road. Not metaphorically, because I rarely do that nowadays, but literally, across the remaining wooden rooftops—and then the slate ones, since uptown is just across the river from here, and the houses keep getting nicer from here on out.

My clever, bare feet know the way, dancing until I can swing from the eaves one-handed, onto the third-story window ledge, to disable a new trap Tom has set on the window.

Well, disable is a bit of an exaggeration. The window catch is easy enough to lift, but it's attached to a wire too inconvenient to clip. I could smash the glass to clip it, but that's clumsy and loud, and there's no telling that there isn't a second wire set to trigger the moment I open the window. Instead, I look for the delivery system.

Ah…. There's a small, wooden straw draining from the lintel above me, something clearly out of place. Cloud poison? Lung fungus? I tear a small, colorful patch from my shirt—I can repatch it later—and stick it in my mouth, soaking the fabric with saliva. I could plug the hole with something, but that generates pressure and there's no guarantee that the plug will hold when I trigger the mechanism. Instead, I tie the patch around the wooden straw like a little nose-bag. In theory, the saliva traps the spores (or poison) while the air is free to pass. I cover my face anyways as I open the window and clamber in. There's a hissing sound, but the "nosebag" does its job.

Tonight there is no bone-saw breath, and no reason to hurry. The house is completely still, and my bag is exactly where I left it.

I relax, just a hair. The house is beautiful, several steps above Number Five on Redemption Alley. Worked wood, diamond-paned windows, display cases and carved molding. It's seen better days, but even in the dark the high ceilings speak to its sense of establishment. Of course, it isn't cozy enough for my tastes.

I poke about the house, double-checking a couple of promising drawers, finding a handful of kings—gold!— and a few bits of cheap jewelry.

Fake-nephew Nori continues to scratch at the door below, and I'm a little surprised at his persistence. A real professional would leave and come back another night with a better plan. Sawing away at the new, fake door will only get him in trouble with the town guard.

I take my time wandering about the house, tripping all the traps I can find. It's good practice. Pale Tom's traps are some of the most intricate I've seen: both well-conceived and elegant. It makes me wonder what the man might have been without the oaths.

I've seen most of them before, scattered through the nicer houses of Ector, through the jobs commissioned by Petri or places visited in desperation. Even a Nightshade has hobbies, I guess. Tom's was, it appears, to place his traps in places he expected me to frequent. I don't understand it; if he'd wanted me dead he could have easily done it. Why the traps?

And he's trapped this place to the gills. Baited surfaces, weight-plates, pitfalls, ankle-wires. . . . There's even a razor in the empty candy bowl. No wonder Petri asked me to raid it again. With all these traps, there's got to be something of value here.

My favorite one is a tarnished wooden box about the size of my hand, the kind that might hold a favorite ring or necklace. It's heavier than it should be, but not by much, and resists being opened, ostensibly because of tarnished hinges. I know better than to force it, though. In acquisitioning, that sort of attitude is a sign of impending retirement.

With a little moonlight, I notice that the tiny "nail heads" all along the southern rim of the box are actually hard, black putty, and they come away easily with a few

82

scrapes of the knife. Beneath each and every bump is a silver glint. Probably 50 little needles all told. I prudently decide to open it with a very unconventional grip. The needles all stab out quickly and retract in a ripple as the lid is fully opened. I open and close it once or twice, and watch the little wave of silver pass around the lower edge of the jewelry box, amazed. A tiny metallic gear in each hinge drives a hidden mechanism.

I'm about to pry the box apart for a better look when I notice the prize. One queenpence. My queenpence.

Only it can't be. I gave that to Petri.

This one is tarnished black, except a tiny pinprick of silver on the regent's face. But it's a message, and I know it's for me. I put it in my pocket.

The magic traps I mostly leave alone. I've always been able to hear that ominous hum that no one else seems to notice.

There's one on a large wardrobe that I do give a try, tossing a wooden mug at it while ducking behind the bed on the other side of the room.

Crack!

The cup explodes.

I try another.

Crack!

Maybe something bigger?

Foom! The chair splatters across the room in a fountain of matchwood.

I chuckle, suddenly guessing that a trap like this could keep an ambitious (and stupid) thief tied up for hours, hoping to wear it out. A dummy trap. The Auctioneers and Collectors are just going to have to deal with this one on their own.

Eventually the soggy spell-books catch my eye. I don't want them, but they aren't the sort of thing that should be left around. Not *those* sorts of spells, anyways. I start a fire in the stone fireplace with the chair I magically dismantled and some spare tinder left on the mantel. This isn't particularly professional, but it is a good joke, and a good acquisitioner never leaves a mess.

The books hiss like demons, and throw off green and purple flames as they burn.

"I dried out your soggy spell-books," I joke to a black-robed specter that isn't really there.

"I'll kill you *and* your lineage," it jokes back.

Urg. Pale Tom's jokes are never funny.

Hungry again, I raid the larder. There's a small sausage in there, which I eat, and several poisoned apples (needle

pricks and bad color), which I don't eat. The scarcity of
food is probably Tom getting back at me for burning his
spell-books. An *eminent* Nightshade should have preserved
calzones, hams, hard cheeses, and expensive wines. But
then I realize *his* larder probably does. This house is only
just a setup.

I'm headed back upstairs when my bare foot brushes a
divot in the larder floorstone, a divot you'd only notice
barefooted. A divot the size of a queenpence.

I get down and feel around it. I put my queenpence in
the divot and it fits perfectly. The stone heats up and
wobbles.

Tom knows I appreciate a well-stocked larder, that I
only wear boots in winter. And I know that Tom loves to
trap things.

I go to the dwindling fire and bring back a firebrand
for light, just in case.

Sure enough, there's a needle—three actually—
protecting this brick, down in crevice holes conveniently
shaped for fingers. I remove them carefully with a pair of
tweezers from my bag and set them to the side.

When I get the brick out, I'm expecting something
valuable. Diamonds would be nice. . . .

Instead, there's a wooden box that rattles a bit when I

shake it. Not diamonds.

I open it carefully, wary of more traps, drying a sappy-looking substance around the latch with some dirt from the hole. A different kind of poison.

The box is filled with rings.

Black rings that swirl on the edges.

Nightshade rings.

I feel sick in my stomach. *Why am I here?* The ring is a rite of passage. Your first kill, your first coercion. Things a Nightshade values. I can feel the power in that box, and it's not something I want.

I try each of them on anyways, feeling sicker and sicker. Each one is dirty, stained with the blood (I assume) of the previous wearer.

Charged with a subtle current, they each play differently on my moods and emotions. Anger. Sadness. Lust. Vengeance. Frenzy. Insanity. None of them crackle like the black ring I stole from the desk upstairs yesterday evening and then lost in the brawl, but they all make my eyesight sharper and my movement swifter.

Not worth the risk. I put them all back in the box and stow the box in my aquisitioner's bag, adding the one from my pocket to the collection. These rings aren't the sort of things you want in the hands of auctioneers and tax-collectors, who are hard enough to avoid as it is.

I don't know what to do with them, but Magnus might, and he definitely won't tell me to pawn them to Petri. . . . As an afterthought, I add the black penny with the silver scratch. It belongs with them.

I've had enough sneaking around for one night. I head back up to the third floor where I made my entrance. It's a little harder to get back on to the roof with a bag tied to my belt, but I manage.

I straighten and run smack into Petri, all set to pounce.

"I thought you might be up here," he chortles, crouching, knife in hand. "Hand over the rings."

"What rings?"

"I know you have them. Sanjuste said you'd go for them."

"You sold me out!" My eyes are pulled to his left hand, to a patch of blackness. Tom's ring. *My* ring.

Petri stops mid-chortle. He's never heard me angry before, and it seems to frighten him.

"Easy, Teacup. Nobody needs to get hurt. I just need to get a box of rings to him and get my debts squared. You know about paying off debts." He laughs, hoping I will, too.

It don't.

"Give them."

I leap past him as his dagger descends, missing me by inches. I'm sliding down one roof and scampering up another, across the Lantern Street "high road" with Petri chasing me. Knowing he's working for Sanjuste gives me new wings. Just one ring in the hands of that monster is unconscionable. If Sanjuste gets hold of just one—the one Petri is wearing, for instance—my family is history.

Petri is faster than I remember him, and rather spry for a man with a damaged leg, but he doesn't know all the tricks, and I can still climb faster. I can see the tiny wall cracks and go up the side of the baker's apartment while Petri's still figuring out how to corner. I've just about left him behind when he does something crazy—a flying leap between two buildings, an attempt to cut me off. He hits the side of the shop instead; it knocks himself out cold.

I stop and go back. I might be able to get Tom's ring, too.

Petri's lying motionless on the ground below, in the middle of a soft herb garden.

Suddenly there are hands grabbing me from behind. I drop to my knees on the rooftop, try to roll sideways, but there are two men behind me, city guards, holding onto my shirt.

I launch myself off the edge, jerking one of them with me. Both let go, one falling on top of Petri, the other teetering in moonlit silhouette. I catch the edge of the roof for a second and then let go, scrabbling down the wall as I fall.

The mud catches me, and I'm up and running. There are voices now, shouting to each other, coordinating, and I realize that I'm in deeper trouble than I thought, even though the clouds have hid the moon again. Thief-hunters. Part of the town guard that I like least. I don't have time to scavenge Petri's ring as they close in. The men at the end of the alley are throwing ropes.

One snares my foot while the others sail harmlessly

past. I kick my leg forward, catching the man by surprise. He grabs his hand where the rope must have burned him. Should have double-wrapped or worn gloves. Amateur.

I'm running, stumbling around another corner, and the crowd is closing fast.

When I head for higher ground, my new tail snags on a nail. I jump back into the group behind me to unsnag it, dashing across a few lightly-armored soldiers, their muscled arms too slow to trap me. The "floor" falls out from under me, but I land four-footed on the ground, splattering mud into the air behind me with my fingers as I leap away. Three strides forward. Rolling under a long-legged guard open-stanced for the tackle.

I jerk sideways and dash down a dark alley, a dead-end planted with vines I know I can scale.

But the vines are gone.

They've been cut away. A trap. Petri brought the guards tonight and left nothing to chance. Like I said, he knows numbers and probabilities, knows what it takes to catch a guy like me.

Excrement.

I turn, dashing back the way I came before they can close it off, frantically grabbing my way up the side of the building, knowing I can only get six feet up.

But they don't know that.

Their line collapses as they anticipate me getting away, and they try desperately to grab me. At the height of my climb, I jump back over them, laying out in the air like a flapping squirrel, watching their hooks and lassos sail past. The last man, the only one to hold his position, tries to catch me and I let him. But I curl into a ball and explode away from him the moment we hit the street. I can feel my small foot pushing the air out of his chest as I surge away.

With guards behind me and the rain on my face, I'm home free.

I don't notice the crutch rising out of the shadows behind a rain barrel until it's too late. It takes me in the shin and I sprawl out on the cobblestone, bag flying from under my belt as my wooden buckle snaps.

Petri is on me in a second, but the best I can do is roll sideways, and I'm pinned. His nose is bloody and he looks really angry. "You shoulda just handed over the box, Teacup. Now I have to give you to the thief-catchers!"

He slides the box of rings out of my bag and into his own cloak while they hobble my hands and feet..

"That murderous bastard killed Sara." I tilt my head back and spit in his face.

He kicks me in the ribs as he gets up. "I was trying to

protect you."

"You're a bag of day-old dog feces," I curse back. "And Sanjuste will be twice as bad as Pale Tom. You think he's going to let you go free?"

This must be a big deal—a *big* deal—for Petri to take me down and use the town guards to do it. I'm his best guy. I always bring him the best stuff. I think about telling the guards that Petri's my fence, but I've got no evidence and he's probably already fed them some line about being the executor of the old lady's will.

The guards are hauling me away, thanks to Petri. I can't hear what they're saying, something about gallows at dawn. I have no doubt that this is another setup: Sanjuste's. I'm the only one who can get into the house, and they played me like a fool.

Fake-nephew Nori, too. They're dragging him away as well, though from the looks and smell of it he wasn't nearly as hard to catch, and has forgotten his change of underwear.

As a courtesy, they knock me out for the trip, after the third time I slip out of my bindings and make a break for it.

93

I wake up in a tiny, wet cell with an urge to pee and a Nightshade hissing through the bars of my dripping window: "*You're* the famous apprentice?"

It's a woman's timbre, silky and quiet. She's crouched on the ground where the cell's bars are, the cell being submerged in the stone footings of the south barracks. The iron-barred window is at eye-level—forehead for me—and her dark shape is blocking out the light of the stars.

I realize that I've been stripped to a pair of peasant trousers, not mine.

"Going to help me out, sister, or just keep hissing like a snake?"

I must be pretty desperate, asking for help from an avowed assassin.

She laughs softly. "Not for an oathless. Maybe if you'd take one to me?"

A phrase drifts through my desperation: "*Some oaths cannot be broken.*"

"No thanks."

"Pity. I can be an exciting teacher." She pulls her hood back for moment so that I can see pale skin and close-cropped red hair. Her lips are scarlet even in the dark, and her shoulders and chest have a promising shape. Young. I realize with a start that she can't be much older than the twins. *Fifteen? Sixteen?*

"How old are you?" I ask.

She shrugs her shoulders—teenage irritation, no masking that—and yanks her hood back up. "Still too young for an apprentice, apparently. Probably better this way."

"Help me anyways," I say softly. "I'm the best in Ector. Slip me a lock pick and I'll make it worth your while." I really don't want to take any oaths, but I don't mind paying in unethical robberies if it will keep my family safe.

She shakes her head wistfully inside the hood. "I find that hard to believe, given your current state. Besides, I was sent to observe and bring back word, not to intervene."

And then she is gone.

Morning comes early and yet I sleep, in spite of intentions to plan my escape, an after-effect of my miserable luck these last 24 hours.

I peer through the bars into the gloomy morning, misty and wet, a morning perfect for death. I can taste it on the air, molding apples and wet hay.

They pull us from our cells, and since shackles don't fit me, I'm tied at the waist to my two guards, men with bony fists and steel-tipped boots to keep me in line.

They parade us out, and post us near the gallows with fake-nephew Nori sniveling and talking to himself quietly. He's cracking.

So am I, I realize. It's the closest I've been to death, and the distance is closing. I wonder when my family will find out.

It isn't long.

Lucinda is up and bustling through the early grocery run. I can see her but she can't see me.

She's perusing the vendor stalls that sprout up every morning between the backside of the church and the blacksmith's shop. Her back is turned, and she's looking at a swatch of white cloth, taking a break from the produce basket under her arm, ignoring the reds, oranges, and greens of fresh produce in the carts around her.

Beautiful, kind Lucinda. If she'd be born anywhere else, she wouldn't have to sigh and place it gently back on the cart.

The vendor sighs too, realizing he's lost another sale.

Lucinda double-takes hard on the execution notice posted on the church wall as she pats the cloth back into place. She can't read, but the sketch of my face spells it out for her. Her hand flies to her mouth in a fountain of carrots, and she's running, running, back toward Redemption Alley. Man, those legs can move.

It's touching. She's never let on that she cared *that* much.

On the other hand, it's scary. I don't want my kids here when they pull the stops and the floor falls out beneath me. I don't want to see tears. I don't want them to see mine hitting the cobblestone right now, or see me chained to the gallows' post.

Of course, the guards take their pretty time. They want a big crowd for their little demonstration of power. They piddle about oiling the trap door, making a few sample drops with potato sacks and the like, tie and then retie the noose. They do a big speech about stealing.

And then they drop fake-nephew Nori. His neck cracks, snapping neatly. Done.

They drone out another speech about the consequences of lawlessness, and then it's my turn.

I feel the splintering planks under my bare feet and look up to see my friends there, staring at me, and my kids, too. Valery is sobbing, wringing her cottony skirt. Timnus is snarling, scowling at Sanjuste, who is also there and looking at Timmy with amusement plain on his face.

Timmy's black look makes me wonder if he's going enlist with the Nightshades just to get revenge.

"It isn't worth it," I mouth to him, but I don't think he understands me.

Magnus has taken last night's bandage from his eyes. It's obvious he can see a little better now, but then again, it's morning, and he could see better yesterday morning, too. There are tears at the corners of his blue eyes, like he's finally seen too much.

"Last words?" The chief executioner barks.

I nod. "I'd like to speak to my priest."

The priest himself looks surprised. I've never been to church in my life. He starts to step forward, unsure.

"Not that one," I mutter to the guard, turning my cheek so I don't offend anyone. "*My* priest. He's from Fortrus Abbey."

The guard looks mildly impressed and a little more

determined. He motions for Magnus, making the sign for last rites.

Magnus mounts the wooden stairs. They creak loudly.

"I can't do anything, Teacup. I'm not ordained, and I don't have Stay of Jurisdiction." He's upset, honest, and his voice is quiet.

I don't waste my time begging. "I was set up, Magnus." It's the truth. "Tom wanted me to find a box of 'retired Oaths' before anyone else did. I'm almost certain of it."

Magnus's voice is low. "Why didn't you tell me sooner? We could have gone to the authorities."

"I just figured it out."

The guard clears his throat, telling us to hurry up, uncomfortable. Hangings that drag out too long get ugly.

"Where are they now?"

I point at Sanjuste.

Sanjuste's eyebrows scrunch together when he sees me pointing at him.

"He's working with Petri. He'll go after Timmy and Val, too."

The big man's face hardens. "Protect the innocent. Bring light to the darkness," he intones.

Whatever.

"And, Magnus?"

"Yes."

"It's my fault you can't see. I put black pomegranate in your drink at the Black Cat."

"Black pomegranate is an antidote for poison."

"I tried to throw the match for my patron."

"And instead you saved my life." His grim face grows darker.

"What?"

"I just realized you haven't had a trial. Eastmarch law requires a trial for capital punishments, with witnesses called. I'll talk to the guards." He puts a hand on my shoulder and I feel a flash of heat shoot up my neck to the crown of my head. "Just in case though, *be strong.*"

I don't bother telling him that the guards have probably been paid off. That's how it works here in Ector. There's no chance of a trial for me.

The guards shake their heads when he asks, one of them glancing sideways at Sanjuste in a tell-tale sort of way.

Tempers flare. Not Magnus's, though. He seems to sag, but argues on until they put hands on him and start dragging him off the platform. It takes four of them, and they are plainly shaken when he threatens them with a

High Tribunal in Upper Ector.

Not that a post-hanging High Tribunal will do me any good.

There is no drum roll or count. The trap drops unexpectedly, and I've only worked one hand free, my lucky hand. I catch the rope above my head to soften the impact on my neck. It helps, but my hand slips, and then I'm hanging hands-free from a hemp ring. I've always been a wiry fellow, but unfortunately there isn't much I can do without air. I can't seem to get my lucky, rope-burned hand into a useful position.

Sanjuste is smug; Petri is looking at his shoes.

The square, the crowd, and the gallows fade, and I apologize to Sara for failing. And to the kids.

I hear Pale Tom chuckling, clouds of laughter around my foggy brain.

"What a lousy apprentice. Never seen a Nightshade die so much."

"I'm not a Nightshade."

Pale Tom only grunts. Or is that my conscious body trying to breathe?

I try again. "I tried to tell him."

"Who?" Tom says.

"Magnus."

"Oh. They only hear what they want to hear."

I wake up with a start, still swinging, my lucky hand wedged between rope-fibers and itching neck.

Barkus emerges from the crowd, huffing and puffing as if he's run all the way from the Black Cat.

"Idiots!" he yells with his stage voice. "You're hanging the only man in Ector who has *ever* stood up to the Nightshades!" For the sake of the argument, he leaves out Magnus and Pale Tom, though they've actually done most of the heavy lifting in that regard. And Pale Tom's not much of an argument, since he *was* Nightshade. But I keep my trap shut. I don't really have a choice. It's awfully hard to breathe, even with a handful of fingers trapped in the rope.

I fade again for a second.

I can't for the life of me get my left hand free from its hog-tie to my waist and feet. If I could do that, I could invert myself and bring my legs into play.

I think of Carmen sewing silk scraps for my burial shroud. Maybe she'll use my stolen banner.

Barkus is arguing forcefully with the Captain of the South Guard who has just arrived, upon hearing about several "irregularities."

"I tell you, he's the real deal. Two nights ago he stuck

103

his knife so deep into Pale Tom LeBlanc that it couldn't be removed, not even for the funeral wrap!"

I worry that Barkus has exaggerated a bit too much, but the crowd seems to like it. "And yesterday morning he took care of one that was coming after his kids. You're going to hang a man who executes Nightshades for a living? Look at him. He's begging you to reconsider!"

I am not. I am begging for a lungful of autumn air.

The crowd, many of them, are shaking their heads in dismay.

The Captain of the Guard looks angry. "This is a question of justice! He was caught breaking and entering the late Widow Pétanque's house on Lantern Street. The Executor of the Will informed us of suspicious behavior, and we were able to apprehend him and recover the stolen goods."

"Stolen goods? Stolen goods!" Barkus spits, looking back at the captain. "James! You know good and well that Pale Tom took up residence in that place the moment the old bat bit the big one. He's the one you should have hanged for stolen goods!"

This is news to Captain James. He looks to his lieutenant, who nods slightly.

Then he snaps back at Barkus, with a little less venom.

"It doesn't change the facts, Barkus. It was still a robbery."

"A search for *evidence*, more likely." Barkus corrects. He turns to the crowd, plays it up just loud enough. "Don't worry, friends. Captain James is a good man. He's not going to kill the Nightshade Slayer." That last bit he says more theatrically.

Captain James winces. "Please don't say that."

"I know, James. . . . I know. . . . You wouldn't want it on your record that you executed a *Nightshade Slayer* without a trial."

"Captain. It's Captain." James can tell he's losing control. He's good, mind you, but he's no match for Barkus.

"Sorry, Captain James. But it's the truth, and the Nightshade Slayer had a deal with old Tom, an inheritance. The old man told me himself that he'd given Slayer his ring."

"That's a conviction, not a help."

"Not when I tell you that's how the two of them killed twenty Nightshades in one night. Right in my own inn."

"Six," the Lieutenant interrupted. "The others were told to leave in peace."

"Seven." Barkus takes control of the narrative. "But it felt like twenty. And this man," he gestures at me, "would've done more if Pale Tom hadn't stopped him."

James's face is incredulous. "You expect me to believe that?"

"Yes. It was all part of the deal, see. Tom wanted Teacup to polish him off at the end of it, make his retirement complete."

Captain James shakes his head, even though the crowd is whispering. They've all heard about the fire and the fight, and this embellishment is going to spread like lice in an orphanage. The Black Cat will be so packed that I'll have to walk across people's heads just to get to my perch, assuming I live that long.

"It's too much. You're a good innkeep, Barkus, but you don't know about law. We've got a thief, and we need to make an example of him."

Barkus stamps his foot. "He and Old Tom had a deal!"

Magnus is looking confused, but Lucinda's telling him to keep his mouth shut, that he's an idiot to start talking about High Tribunals right now. One wrong word will put an end to me. It only takes one good arrow. I can even see a few archers eyeing me lazily from the barracks roof, begging me to do something stupid. I don't. As long as I stay on the gallows I should be fine.

That doesn't mean I need to be *hanging* from them.

Pop! My other hand slips free.

I flex it a few times to get the blood moving, then position both hands above my head and invert myself slowly to get the weight off my neck. It feels so wonderful, along with the gulps of air, that I climb up the rope backward, using my feet to help, careful to leave the noose in place. I sit on the top of the scaffolding to watch the drama of my hanging unfold.

The archers flex their bows, so I decide not to push my luck, except to swing my feet jauntily in the open air.

There are impressed whispers in the crowd. Okay, so I am showboating a little, but it might be my last chance.

Barkus's gift is just as rare, and Sanjuste has made a mistake by letting the man talk. The innkeep can spin a whole world in just a few sentences and he's doing it now, knitting a tale about assassins and Tom and hopes and dreams. The thief sketcher, now execution sketcher, seems to have caught the flavor. He's drawing frantically with a charcoal, while the captain continues to argue with Barkus and another squad of guards brings out the chopping block on a two-man handcart, since the noose is obviously not good enough for the mighty Nightshade Slayer.

The chopping block is a big, nasty black-oak thing that

would turn the river crimson for a day if you managed to heave it in. It's generally saved for special occasions, but I guess they want to test it on my neck, since the rope wasn't enough. It's a nice gesture to know I might get to add my blood to royalty and foreign marshals.

Suddenly there's a commotion. Valery is chatting up the guards, getting in the way of the cart without making it obvious, showing them her new boots, turning her ankle for admiration. It's obviously a sales pitch. She motions for Timmy to demonstrate the finer points of the boots, and as he bends over one hand flits near the cart's wheel while the other flourishes near some complicated stitching, and a little too much leg. I'm going to have a talk with Lucinda about that. Maybe.

The guards wave them off angrily and they scamper back to Carmen, who sews them up in a gigantic hug.

I smile as I realize Timmy knows a wheel-pin is important. Or maybe Lucinda told him. I can't tell. She nods curtly at him thirty seconds later, though, when the cart's wheel falls off in the middle of the square and the head-block tumbles down onto the cobblestone. It's heavy, and no amount of grunting will get it back into the sabotaged cart, or the back-up cart, and no one in the gathering crowd will help them lift it now. Not even Sanjuste, who is pushing his way from the crowded square.

The people push back of course. They all want to crowd in close to hear the drama.

And then Lucinda is standing next to Petri, arguing with him as he presses something into her palm. Magnus is smiling, because there's a courier on a horse headed for the gallows, waving a Cease-and-Desist order over his head. A flustered Captain James doesn't know it yet, but this execution has just kicked the bucket.

The weirdest part is how Lucinda catches up with Sanjuste just as he breaks from the crowd. Her hand darts in and out of his pocket.

I get excited, thinking Petri has tipped her off, but her

hand comes away empty, no handful of rings to show for her effort. I know because her face is white as she melts back into the crowd.

The messenger from Northgate finally gets his message across as the crowd turns to watch him canter up, people diving to get out of the way.

"This man is not to be hanged!"

"Why not?" Captain James replies with resignation.

"For the confirmed elimination of a bountied Nightshade, one Kinkaid Lumière of Doward. This man is the honored recipient of the Lady Selwin's congratulations!"

"See! See!" Barkus and his large, round belly bounce with fervor.

Lucinda is urging him to stop with a one-handed, off-with-your-head slitting motion. I wish she wouldn't do that almost as much as I want Barkus to shut up.

But a good story in motion is a hard thing to stop, and Barkus has the bit in his mouth like a horse running for the stable.

"And I tell you, just yesterday Teacup was in my inn promising a big clean-up to come, how all those doers of evil better run for cover. He even threatened me, bless him. But I don't blame him. Sometimes it's hard to know."

Barkus takes a hard stare at Sanjuste, and when he can't find him, looks to Petri. *You're next.*

It's too much for the guards. The honest ones have been chomping at the bit for a champion, and the dishonest ones can admit to themselves that fewer Nightshades would be better.

The final straw falls when the sketcher shows his newly drafted pardon poster:

"Teamus Steaps, yor Nightshade Hunter."

The drawing has a pile of black-cloaked Nightshades dead at my feet, remarkably well rendered. Hell and Damnation. And Pan's Beard. I'm a dead man.

After that, they get me off the gallows fast, bowing and shaking my hand, apologizing. Complimenting me on my climbing abilities. Looking worried.

"Are you okay, Mister Steeps?"

"I'm fine."

"A drink, perhaps?"

"No thanks. Prefer to drink from a known source."

"Well thought, sir. It would take more than a little gallows to finish *you* off, Mr. Steeps."

"Of course." I say it quietly because my throat feels

scratchy.

"Do you need any assistance, Mr. Steeps?

"Yes, I do. I'd like to talk to the sketcher." Pan's beard, this is a pain. As if it isn't bad enough to have a gigantic, red target painted on my chest now, for all the deadliest killers in Teuron.

The sketcher steps up, older than I'd guessed, hair dyed recently as evidenced by the charcoal stain on his scalp.

"Nicely done, sir," I say.

"What can I do for you, Slayer. Anything."

"It's pretty easy. Can you fix my surname? S. T. E. E. P. S." When I'm perfectly dead next week, I'd like for them to at least get my bloody tombstone spelled correctly.

The sketcher relaxes. "Right away, sir!"

Someone in the crowd is selling meat pies. The smell of golden pastry and spiced lamb hits me like one of Magnus's meaty fists. My stomach grumbles loudly, because they don't serve breakfast to the condemned. That would be a waste of good porridge.

A gap-toothed villager, the same idiot who tipped off the brawl, is bragging about how this all started when someone got jealous about the gorgeous barmaid that kept hanging around his table.

"Yeah right, George! Prob'ly 'cause yer didn't pay yer bill!

"Yer a lout!" George retorts.

"Yer double!"

A small scuffle ensues.

Barkus seizes the moment, turns to Captain James. "Mr. Steeps will be in touch. No small jobs, please. Only the most serious. He's had a hand in the death of over 20 assassins to date, so let's not waste his time."

He's pulling me down the stairs, with Magnus following in his wake, my family closing in. "You better run straight to Fortrus Abbey," Barkus whispers.

"Did you have to finish that story?" I complain.

"I got a little carried away." His cheeks are flushed and he looks healthier from his early morning run to the gallows. "I know you ain't really aiming to shut them Nightshades down. And I'm sorry for all the trouble I've made for ya."

"You bought me time. You saved my life. Thanks." I stare Barkus straight in the eye, for a full minute till he knows I'm thankful. He looks worried, over his thick stubble and strong shoulders and large stomach, and I know immediately how this story needs to finish, even if I have no intention of seeing it through. It needs to end with hope.

"Barkus, if the Nightshades have anything to fear, it's me." I say it in my soft voice, because I've never had much bravado to begin with, and always had to tiptoe around that. "Especially if they come 'round my house again."

Barkus's eyes go wide. He thinks I'm serious.

"You still better run."

"I know."

There's one last oddity. A girl with short, red hair is watching me closely from the middle of the crowd. She isn't wearing black, but I know it's her, and we're not moving fast enough. She cuts off our escape without making it obvious that she's doing it. But I know.

I'm looking for a weapon when she greets us in a civil tone.

"Handsome, sir," she says in her silky voice, brown eyes glittering. "If I can ever be of assistance. . ."

I glare at her. "Some assistance last night might have been nice."

Carmen catches up with us, and the twins are right behind. "Teacup, who is your *friend*?" Her tone says something, but I'm not quite sure what.

"Someone interested in watching me hang."

Red's sly satisfaction slips for a second. "I was sent to

115

observe . . ."

Carmen threads her arm through mine. "How about observing us walk away?"

We split apart a few blocks from Redemption Alley. We all agree it's best the kids and I leave Ector early tomorrow with Magnus, if we can get a coach. The ladies will watch the house with a pair of Northgaters standing guard. Neither look happy about this arrangement, but Carmen isn't ready to leave her clients behind and Magnus is insistent that Lucinda stay in Ector to keep Carmen company.

Carmen slips a thimble into my pocket for good luck before following Magnus toward the liveries. She touches my arm lightly and looks away just as quickly. "I have a friend there. He can help," she says.

Lucinda just stomps away to get the food Barkus has pledged for getting us on the road quickly, growling something about using her dagger on Magnus. Valery stomps after her, obviously taking behavioral notes.

Timnus lingers, though he's supposed to go with Lucinda. "Da, I want to stay in Ector with Lucinda and Carmen." His eyes are both mischievous and hopeful. "I'll spread word about the town that you're out on business and won't be back for several months. Things will be safer for the ladies that way."

"That's a good idea." I know there's more. "And?"

117

"And people are going to come running to buy my shoes, now that we're back in business."

This is the part where I tell him, like a father, how things are going to go down: as safely as possible. None of my kin are staying in Ector while Sanjuste is on the loose.

"You can make shoes for the monks," I say in consolation.

"Monks are boring."

"Boring like Magnus?"

That catches his imagination.

"You're going to have to work on your sizing, though," I say pointing to Valery's clompy impression of Lucinda.

Timnus flashes me his "do-I-look-stupid?" grin. "Da! If I made boots that fit her to the inch, I'd be making her new boots every day!"

"Just checking," I recover. Smart kid.

I change subjects to seal the deal. "Still got that wheel-pin?"

His grin widens into something genuine as he pulls it from his pocket.

"What are you going to do with it?"

"I dunno, Da. Save it for luck?"

"Good plan. Mind Lucinda."

He scampers off, stuffing the pin back into his pocket.

I don't go directly into the house, which the kids have forgotten to lock again. I don't blame them, for all the excitement that's been going around. Instead, I sit on the back steps for a long while, enjoying the fresh breeze, the sudden freedom, and the happy thought of raising kids. Being almost-dead makes being Dad more precious.

When I start feeling sleepy, I go inside and head up the stairs. Last night's adventure is catching up with me.

I'm yawning in my own kitchen when I realize I'm not alone. There are boots on my table, and the owner of those boots is grinning like a skeleton.

The smell of improperly cured shoe-leather drifts through the air. "Sanjuste."

I leave off the honorific. Sanjuste's no master of the trade, no matter what the guildmen say (probably out of fear).

He's a beast of a man, at least two boots taller than me, and several times as thick. And he's gained weight since the last time I had the misfortune of gazing upon him. I've compared him to Magnus before, but today he looks thicker in the middle, decidedly pear-shaped, thickening in girth around the waist, not unlike Barkus. He doesn't strike me as big today so much as fat, but I know that girth can move quickly for his size. When he bounces up from his double-reinforced cobblers bench, you'd better already be moving, if you want to stay out of the way.

But I stand my ground, at least for the moment. "Get out of my house."

"I told you to keep a close eye on your kids." A wicked grin spreads across his face.

He wants me to think he's found them, but I know better. I know for a fact they're hale and hearty, helping Lucinda and Magnus.

121

I'm afraid, but only a little. Sanjuste leaves his dirty work to Frank, or so I've heard, and the back door is just a scamper away.

Creak. Clack.

The sound of someone barring my own door below. A glance tells me it's Frank.

Fear creeps in. They must have come straight here after the execution. "I'm opening up the shoe shop again," I say, sliding away from the stairway and Frank's long narrow rope. It wouldn't be strong enough to hang Magnus, but it'll do quite well for me. "You're going to wish you never came here."

His grin spreads wider. He peers around as if to mock my lack of allies. "You won't be opening up anything."

I'm not stupid. They're here to kill me, and not in the quick and silent way of Nightshades. They're here to make me suffer. They're here to make a mess and send a message. By now everybody has seen Val's new boots, and there were at least three people in the gallows crowd wearing Timmy's trademark, which I didn't recognize until this morning. Those two have been selling shoes for the last two weeks, and I didn't know anything about it!

But it's time to cut my losses and get out. I wouldn't put Magnus up against these two, not in such a tight space, not with him still half-blind and such. I surely don't have a chance.

Sanjuste springs forward without warning, but I'm faster. To the kitchen window. It's big enough for me, but not big enough for him. On the roof I can lock the door and set fire to the house. It'll be a shame, but I can't afford to have this monster out and about.

Only the window won't budge, and I don't have time to find out why. I leap to the side, narrowly avoiding a crashing blow from his right hand, and a leather-punching awl it has brought along. The sharp awl settles into the wood and sticks, buying me a half-second to dash to the master bedroom door.

Locked, and no time for lock-picks.

I feel a cold sweat, watching Frank as he guards the stairs. They've been planning for this. The window is nailed shut and the bedroom door is locked. We never do that. Between Timnus, Valery, and me, we all know the uselessness of locks. Except now. Now they're a big deal. And no one is due back for another hour or two.

It's the end of the line for me. Unless I can play them against each other, they're going to catch and kill me, and it's going to be messy.

Frank steps back into the stairwell as if hearing my

thoughts, getting out of Sanjuste's way.

They watch me as realization sets in, and Sanjuste smiles a cruel smile. "I told you I didn't like you seven years ago. I told you this wasn't the right side of town to set up shop on. I told your precious wife, too. You think your blind, little Paladin's going to keep you safe? Not when I have Tom's collection."

He flexes a meaty fist, one holding a pair of leather snips. Five black rings, one for each finger on his left hand, even his thumb. All the same, all different. I can see swirls in them, now that they've been cleaned, like the folds in Tenebrus's own coat, swirls that keep moving like a cloak flapping in the wind, or a dark cloud roiling up a thunderstorm.

I play for time. "How you make shoes with those paws is beyond me," I say.

He scowls.

"Oh. Right. Not well, I remember now. My son is going to rip your business apart."

Sanjuste's scowl deepens. "Your boy was lucky. Frank's an idiot and slow. We'll catch him one of these days. Hell, we may even get to string him up next to you."

Frank just grins.

I lose my cool. I'm not a fighter but I go for Sanjuste,

with the same knife I put into poor Pale Tom. I take him by surprise, but it barely grazes him as he pivots out of my way. Suddenly I'm trapped in a smelly armpit. I can see a small strong rope coming over my head.

"Wait till his darling kids see him dangling from the rafters," Sanjuste laughs.

Frank laughs, too. It's a stupid laugh. A trollish laugh.

My chest tightens. I point my knuckles and jab hard in Sanjuste's ribs, but there's too much fat protecting the soft parts. I squirm. I bite. But Sanjuste holds me tight until Frank's hoisting me towards my own rafters. I'm holding Sanjuste by the shirt to stay on the ground, but he aims his leather snips at one of my fingers. "This little piggy . . ."

I move my fingers, hear Pale Tom sighing. "All that hard work wasted. Ector will have Sanjuste as its Nightshade. . . . I should have picked Lucinda. She's so much more clever."

What would Lucinda do?

Check the pockets, I realize. Sanjuste could be carrying anything. A dagger. A shiv. A cobbler's pick.

My hand finds the right pocket just as Frank heaves-to again. My fingers close around something circular. Tom's ring flashes hot in my hand, and I know suddenly that Petri gave it to Lucinda and Lucinda planted it, in case

125

Sanjuste proved himself devious and managed to catch me unawares.

And then I'm airborne. But now I have an ally.

I can feel time slow again, can feel the rotation of the rope, can sense the movement of Frank behind me as I turn, can smell his foul breath as he hoists me toward the rafters. My timing is perfect as I deliver a heel to Frank's ear and the soft part behind it. Frank crumples, dropping me. My feet punch the floor.

Hello, planking.

I can't get more than three fingers between the noose and my neck before Sanjuste's got me off the ground again, keeping a distance from my flailing feet. I'm still going to choke; it's just going to take a little longer. I fight it.

"You always were a tricky little bastard," he swears. "I should have handled this ages ago."

He doesn't know that I have my ring, that I can hear his muttering even though I should be passing out, or that I can hear the scratching in the attic of someone coming through my trapdoor. (So that's how they've been getting in!)

I stop kicking to save air.

I hear Timnus and Valery whispering frantically,

arguing.

"Lucinda said wait!" Timnus is pleading. "She's getting Magnus."

"We don't have time, Timmy! They've got *Da* in there. They're killing him."

Sanjuste has tied off the rope and is kicking Frank, who isn't waking up. Probably should be putting a knife in me instead, but I don't remind him. Darkness seems to gather around him, but he doesn't hear the sounds in the attic. I guess that's not a skill every Nightshade has, not even one with five rings.

I spin round and round, and Val is there, in the rafters, trying to cut me down. I scream in my head *Get away! Get away, Val!* but the words get caught on the rope around my throat. She can't hear anything but her own panic.

Sanjuste throws his knife at—one of several he's laid out on the table—sinks it straight into her delicate side. She screams and falls, bleeding. My tears fall with her.

I grab the rope with my free hand, trying to kick up, frantic, and feel Sanjuste's enormous hand catch my foot and yank it back down.

"Watch with me," he says cruelly.

He's still watching her twist and turn on the floor when Timmy pounds a leather awl straight through the

127

man's right boot, foot, and floor, pinning it in place. I don't know where he came from, but seeing his taller, braver sister bleeding is all the incentive he needs. Then he swings a chair, hammering it into the huge shoe-maker's chest.

The back door shudders below, and Sanjuste's knee sends Timmy sprawling, out cold.

Magnus bursts through the door, snatching up Valery and pulling her to safety. There's a flash of light, and then he's bleeding for her, gasping, placing a hand to his side. Stanching blood flow.

Sanjuste curses, striking out, but his boot is still pinned to the floor and he can't reach Magnus, who anticipates what's coming next. Magnus twists sideways, reaches past Sanjuste's other knife, his fingers bent in a long-fist. His reach and his good form make it possible to connect from a distance and there's a crunching sound as Sanjuste's nose surrenders.

I'm still dangling by my neck from the noose, but gratefully my hands have kept the knot from closing too much. I manage a kick to Sanjuste's swaying head before I pass out.

I'm in a pale-green field of feather-grass with an old man dressed in black.

"How touching! Another visit from my failed apprentice. I really should have just let that barmaid pickpocket me!" But the fool's grinning like he's forgotten to be dead.

I wake up to the most beautiful sight. Timnus and Valery staring at me, foreheads worried.

Carmen is nearby, her face flooding with relief when she sees my eyes open. "Teamus. Stop trying to get away from me."

My head spins a little, either from the blood-loss or the blood-rush to my cheeks, I can't exactly calculate.

They keep asking me how many fingers they're holding up, dumbest question ever.

"Thirteen?" I mumble.

"Da-aa-aa!"

It's the tone they take when they know I'm joking.

Lucinda leans over and whispers in my ear. Her voice is serious and a little sad. "Reverse grip works well. From behind."

When I press her for details, she shakes her head. "I did what had to be done. Everyone else was unconscious or headed there, and that monster had Magnus by the throat. I'm sorry we didn't come sooner."

At dinner, Magnus pulls out a chair for Lucinda. He's being awful nice to her. Too nice.

I mean to warn him about it privately, but he beats me to the punch. "What's this about rings in Ector?"

Lucinda, Carmen, and Valery exchange surreptitious looks, and then concentrate extra on their food. Timmy's eyes go wide.

"I'm not really sure," I blush.

He knows I'm not being straight with him. He's learned that much at least.

I sigh, giving in. "Show a little courtesy to a girl in Ector and it means you like her. Show enough courtesy and she might give you a ring. Show *too much* courtesy and the law might agree to her claim on you. Don't ever be in that boat, Magnus, not unless you mean it."

Magnus doesn't seem convinced. "All men and women have claim on my courtesy. I'm not supposed to treat people poorly just because it might incur obligations."

"You don't know what you're talking about, Magnus."

"Of course I do," he protests. "I'm not afraid of obligation. Life is obligation—to the righteous."

"Are you afraid of marriage?"

That shuts him up. It's obvious that he likes Lucinda,

132

and equally obvious that he has absolutely no experience with women.

Silence at the table. Tense chewing.

"Hang on," he says. "You mean to tell me that if I'm too nice to Lucinda, she might have a binding marital claim?" He seems both horrified and piqued by the prospect.

"Out with it, Magnus."

And then I see what he's hiding under the table.

"Magnus. What is that in your hand?"

"It's a ring."

"I can see that."

"Lucinda gave it to me. She says my hair sets off the gold. Says it was her dad's."

He has the look of a whipped puppy that knows it's peed somewhere it shouldn't. Magnus is smart about some things—fighting, for instance—but he can be so simple.

"I told you not to accept any jewelry in Ector!"

Lucinda scowls at me, suddenly indignant. She knows the customs in Ector, and how to use them to her advantage. Maybe Solange is different, but in Ector—and all of Eastmarch for that matter—we know commitment. We may not be perfect, but if you can get us to commit to anything then it might as well be carved in stone. And

Magnus has just made a huge commitment.

"It fits perfectly," he defends.

"Of course it does!" I say. "She's been sizing you every time she checks the scabs on your knuckles."

Now Lucinda looks surprised.

"Don't look so surprised, Lucy."

She blushes at a nickname Barkus invented for her years ago, but uses rarely..

"You know me better than to think I'd miss a detail like that," I say.

But the surprises aren't over yet. Like I said, Magnus isn't stupid, he just needs experience to connect all the dots. And now he's got it.

"Wait," he says. "What about you and Carmen? You've been awfully nice to her lately."

I blush. "That's different. We're friends. We've known each other for a long time."

"Lucinda and I are friends."

"And your ring says you're 'committed' to her. Committed. You're practically married. All you need now is a quiet—"

"Hang on," he says cutting me off. "So you haven't gotten a ring from Carmen? You're not due for one of these 'committed' rings?"

Suddenly I'm glad we're leaving tomorrow. "I . . . uh . . .well . . .That's a good question for tomorrow." My scalp prickles and I try to excuse myself, but the rest happens too fast, even for me.

"Don't move," Carmen blurts. "I made you something."

I can't move now if I wanted to. It's like I've been glued to my chair with pine sap.

She leaves the table and rushes to her sewing chest. "I was saving this for tomorrow, but now seems like the perfect moment." She hands me a pair of neatly-folded leggings. They look soft, comfortable, and silent—the kind that don't even whisper while moving across rooftops. Her secret project. It's what she's been working on in the evenings, what she's been hiding in her wooden box.

They're beautiful.

Lucinda smirks. "Look at that grin. See? I told you he'd like them."

"Da, aren't you going to try them on?" Val's eyes jump sideways to Carmen and back to me, smiling.

I can see the impression of a ring somewhere in the fabric, in a secret pocket that she knows I can find, but clever still. She wants commitment. "Give me a minute, Val. Trying on a new pair of pants is not a thing to rush

135

into."

Timnus giggles. "You're not making any sense, Da!"

There's a rapping at the door, like Redemption Alley has become the newest tavern now that Nightshades are falling left and right. Magnus, Timmy, and I all scramble to get it. Magnus's sight seems to be getting better and better. He only trips over one stool in his haste to help me answer the door.

I open the spy hole and glimpse a gap-toothed man in a cloak. One I know well. One who returned my ring. Petri has his usual sour look, with his hands out in the open where I can see them.

I open the door slowly. There are no apologies, no groveling. For Petri, even being here is an apology, a bending of stinging pride. He hands me a black queenpence. "It was the only thing in the box that Sanjuste didn't want. Thought it might be important."

"Thanks." It's Tom's penny, from the pin-box. There's a little more silver on the face of it. Two pinpricks, like Petri's been trying to polish it. "Thanks," I say again.

"I seen what you did to Sanjuste. This town's going to sleep a lot easier from now on."

I don't tell him it was Lucinda. I just nod.

"If anyone deserves that ring, Teacup, it's you," he

says after a long pause. "That one's different than the others. And you're going to need it. They've put a bounty on your head, no doubt."

"Thank you," I choke out. "You saved my life."

Petri says nothing for long seconds, eyes shifting from me to Magnus to Timmy.

I can see he's favoring his bad leg again. "Do you want it back? You. . . ."

Petri shakes his head. "Stupid, no. It won't fix my leg. It won't make me better at things I'm not good at."

"How do you know?" I ask.

Petri's nose twitches, raising one side in a half snarl. "'Cause I still can't climb a drainpipe."

"You were faster than I've ever seen you."

"Teacup, get it through your thick skull. It helps everyone like that. Sneaking. Running. Hiding." He pauses. "Killing. But it pours its soul into what you're already good at, and you're a natural. Except maybe the killing part."

"And you?"

"Not those things. I'm good at countin', and I don't need any extra help. Now I know exactly how many steps it takes to get from home to the Black Cat, from the Black Cat to the docks, from the docks to the fish market, from the fishmarket to your house. . . . Pan's mangy beard! I'm

137

already good at numbers, I don't need all that extra garbage bouncing around in my head. And I made Barkus cry."

He laughs his mean laugh. Some things don't change.

"It was funny. Big, fat tears. Sobs. Couldn't talk for ten minutes, kept saying you wouldn't last ten days."

Then he scowls at me, assuming I have my ring in my pocket. "Get that thing away from me. I don't need help being mean, either."

I shrug and tilt my head, by way of invitation. "Want to come up?"

"Nah-h, Teacup. I've got better things to do tonight."

All the same, he stares wistfully up the stairs. "Is Carmen there?"

I nod.

He nods back. "Good."

He pushes his tongue through his pearlies and makes a soft whistle. "If you ever have any goods you want to move," he says finally, "you know where and when to find me. Just don't try to slip me another of those Pan-cursed rings." Then he's down the back steps and into the square, hobbling on a new crutch, one that looks suspiciously like Magnus's old sword.

Magnus is smiling, watching him go.

138

"Da, I'm hungry."

"Good point, Timmy. Who knows when the coach is going to get here. Let's eat."

We head back up the risers to food, friends, and commitment, hoping that the door stays un-knocked for a good, long while.

Or at least for one night.

If I hadn't been so exhausted I might have noticed the note scritching between the threshold and the door.

About the Author

Benjamin K. Hewett is a NASA Program Analyst who lives in Houston and chases numbers for a living, though he'd rather be writing fiction. In graduate school, he won 3rd Place in the Mayhew Short Story Contest and continues to write short stories amid larger novel projects. Ben also enjoys playing with his three kids, coaching soccer, and juggling fire. He has a BA in French and a Master's Degree in Public Administration, both from BYU. To stay informed about upcoming sequels, subscribe to Ben's newsletter or follow his blog at BKHEWETT.COM.

About the Illustrator

Marta Maszkiewicz is a Warsaw-based artist specializing in the fantasy and fairy-tale genres. She creates art for books, advertisements, and computer games. When not at work, she can be found reading, gaming, doing traditional Indian dance, or serving the whims of her very own cat. Marta also has a degree in architecture, which she carefully avoids using.

35176319R00081